MW00386914

HIGH ROLLAZ

Andre L. Simpson

Copyright © 2018 by Andre L. Simpson All rights reserved. No part of this book may be reproduced or used in any manner without written permission of the copyright owner except for the use of quotations in a book review. For more information, address:
andrelsimpson37@gmail.com

I would like to express my special thanks of gratitude to my son Andre-Joshua, to my daughter Siroya, and my parents for always believing in me during my journey as a writer.

Contents

Drew was your average 20yr old college sophomore, a ladies' and a family man from a middle-class home. All this would change upon meeting Abdul, Kendu and Clark. After being introduced to an illegal lifestyle of committing robberies and selling drugs, he becomes addicted to the fast pace life, at the same time keeping his family in the dark about his illegal enterprise. During all this he is faced with many odds: being a successful student, a husband, a father at 20yrs old and being a Drug Kingpin. He endures many losses as people within his circle end up dying because of these illegal activities and, at the same time, this causes him to unleash the demon within him that he never knew existed. What lies at the end of the road for Drew? Only time will tell.

Chapter 1

It was a relatively quiet evening in Stony Brook. Sitting in bed on a Friday night bored playing Madden, trying to figure out my next move. Being in a town filled with numerous colleges, I knew there had to be something going on. My cell phone started ringing and immediately jarred me from my thoughts. At first, I was puzzled because the ring tone was unfamiliar, but when I looked at the screen I realized who it was. It was this African dude I met earlier this week in my Econ class by the name of Abdul. I was curious to see what was up so I answered.

"Hello, who dis?"

"It's me, Abdul" he replied

"Oh aight, I kinda figured it was you but I wasn't too sure about the phone number" I lied.

"What are you getting into tonight?"

"Nothing as of right now, why, do you have something in mind? I'm definitely trying to go hang out with some sexy ladies, especially after all these damn mid-terms."

"Oh aight, well me and a couple friends were planning on heading to this spot in Brooklyn. I know the bouncer so we can get in with ease, and it's free for females, so you know it's gonna be jam packed with some fine ladies.

"That definitely sounds enticing, is there any kind of dress code or age limits?"

"There isn't any dress code and the age limit is 18 and over. Matter of fact, I might need you to do the driving, if you don't mind."

"Why, what's wrong with your car?"

"All four of us won't be able to fit. If you're not feeling it, just let me know. It's not a problem."

I thought about his statement for a quick second. By the way he came at me with the offer, it sounded as if I was his only way to the club. Right then I thought, I ain't got nothing else doing, so what the hell. "K, I'm in, but you all got to chip in for gas and tolls", I stated in a stern tone.

"That shouldn't be a problem, Drew. More or less, that was a given."

We agreed that everyone would meet up at his apartment and leave from there. Most second, third and final year students chose to get off-campus apartments, mainly to avoid the hassles of campus rules and regulations. For me being in my second year, it was ideal to get an apartment off campus, and at the same time it made me popular with the ladies. After the phone call ended, I stopped playing the video game and decided to get ready. I went to take a shower and pick out what I was wearing. I always considered myself a classy dresser so I felt that anywhere I went I had to be well put together. I stood at a magnificent 6ft 2inches tall, with dark caramel complexion and was solidly built at 200lbs. It was now the end of March and the temperature relatively stayed in the 50's and 60's, so tonight I opted to throw on a white Lacoste polo, Diesel jeans and a pair of blue Prada Kicks with the jacket to match. No one could have told me I wasn't looking fly. Moments later I left my apartment heading to Abdul's to get the fellas. Upon my arrival I called to let them know I was downstairs waiting. As they exited the apartment and headed towards my car, I saw Abdul with two other dudes in tow. The other two guys he was with looked familiar but I just couldn't pinpoint where I'd seen them before. When they got in the car, Abdul introduced them to me as Clark and Kendu. Looking at them, they appeared to be complete opposites. Clark seeming to be no more than about 5ft 9inches, approximately 180lbs and dark complexion, while Kendu was about 6ft 4inches", with light brown skin and weighed about 215lbs. We all greeted each other with daps, showing mutual respect for one another, before pulling off heading for Brooklyn. A conversation was initiated by Abdul regarding the females on campus that he has been with and was trying to get with. He went on to mentioned this chick name Clevita he was trying to fuck; which caused us to all erupt in laughter.

"What the hell is so funny about that?" he asked looking dumbfounded.

We all replied, one after the other.

"Yo son, Shorty is a straight freak. I think you the only dude on campus that ain't been there before." I stated laughing my ass off.

"Oh word son? That's crazy because I have been trying for a while to get with her and every time I try to make a move or be romantic in any way she turns me down."

"Bro, don't allow her to play you out like that, she's the easiest piece of ass on campus. Her name should be changed to 'legs wide open'" I said letting out a loud chuckle.

Clark then turned to me and asked "Drew, do you smoke weed?"

I replied "Yea, why? What's good?"

"I got some Blueberry haze on me, so I wanted to know if you would mind me smoking in your car." Clark asked.

"Bro, you better stop playing and spark that shit" I replied ejecting the cigarette lighter out of its consul and passing it to him.

For the remainder of the ride we kept on puffing weed, acting a fool, cracking jokes and reciting the rhymes of songs on the radio. When Drake and Lil Wayne's hit 'Good Kush and Alcohol', came on everyone in the car went crazy, singing along. "I don't know what I would do without y'all, ima ball til the day I fall". The topic of our conversation soon transitioned to narcotics. We spoke about who had what and who held weight until Kendu exclaimed "Yo son, we don't even pay for our weed."

His comment caught my attention immediately so I asked "What the hell are you talking about?"

"It's simple, my dude. We just find out who has it, find a way to connect with them and set up a deal, then take whatever they got; it's nothing. As easy as Doh, Rae, Me." He replied with a sinister smile.

Clark then turned to me and chimed in "Drew, if you're trying to get down to make some easy paper just let me know, we could always use an extra hand."

"Aight bro, ima definitely think about it and let you know."

CHAPTER 2

About an hour had passed before we finally made it to the club. By the look of the line outside, leading all the way around the corner with all of the beautiful women waiting to get in, I knew I was definitely in for some fun. I drove around the block in search of parking until Abdul spotted someone getting ready to pull out of a spot. I made sure to move quickly so no one else could get the spot before I did. After exiting the car, we scurried to the club. We only waiting in line for about 5 minutes, but as soon as we entered I thought to myself, that the hour trip to the club was more than worth it.

Mavado ft. Nicki Minaj's club banger 'Give it All to Me' was blazing through the speakers and had the entire club in a frenzy. The building was jam packed with patrons filling every available spot. The DJ booth was elevated, with girls dancing in all types of sexy lingerie to the sounds echoing from the speakers. This was the first time I had ever seen anything like this; no wonder Abdul was so eager to hit this spot. We strolled pass the dance floor on the way to the bar and saw that it was completely packed to capacity with club patrons getting their groove on. Right away I saw a couple eye candies I intended on getting at before the night was over, but opted not to as yet, so we continued on our way to the bar to get something to drink. I wasn't much a fan of drinking, so I settled for a Heineken while everyone else went all out buying bottles of Ciroc Vodka and Hennessy V.S.O.P.

Seeing this I thought to myself, "These dudes are really doing numbers. Either that or they were frontin' their asses off trying to stunt. Moments later we decided to split up but agreed that we wouldn't leave any one from the group, unless that person had a girl with a ride lined up for the night. Right about then the weed mixed with the liquor began to take effect, causing all my inhibitions to go out the window. Both Clark and Kendu had disappeared into the crowd, leaving me stuck with Abdul. I then made my way in the direction of the dance floor to find a dance partner with Abdul in tow. It was now the reggae hour so the DJ was blazing back to back smash hits by the top names in the industry. Being from the islands, dancing came natural to me, so I always used it as a magnet for the ladies. With my dance moves and my good looks, it was never hard to get whoever or whatever I wanted. Abdul, on the other hand, was a totally different story. He was skinny as hell with a thick Somalian accent and a humongous head the size of a watermelon, with a bald spot to compliment it. Not to mention he was only 5ft 6 tall; but you couldn't tell him he wasn't all that, because he'd curse you out for hating on him. He was obviously stuck in denial. He also seemed to be in his late 30s and looked totally out of place in college, but if you ever asked him his age, he would tell you he was only 20 years old. As soon as I stepped onto the dance floor, my attention was drawn to a sexy Latina with one of the phattest asses I have ever seen; the rest of her body complimenting it oh so well. I realized she wasn't alone, but I was determined to get with her regardless of that. I cautiously made my way over to her, whispering in her ear. "May I have this dance?" while pressing my body up against hers, causing my nature to rise. Before answering, she turned around looking me up and down smiling; then she turned back around moving her hips in a winding motion providing me with a desired response, *"As long as you can keep up."* Mad Cobra's hit song *'Flex'* came through the speakers as we danced, grinding up on each other. I could tell that Shorty was feeling me because my dick kept on bulging through my pants the entire time and she just intensified her movements even more, grinding up on me as if she didn't feel a thing. Thinking that this was the right moment and possibly my only chance before we had to part, I whispered, "What's your name Ma?"

"It's Jasmine", she replied with a smile.

"That's a pretty name. Where are you from, if you don't mind me asking?"

"Nah, not at all, I am actually from Upstate, New York"

"Oh, word? So what are you doing all the way in the City?"

"I go to school in Long Island, Old Westbury to be exact, what about you?"

"That's actually a coincidence because I'm also from Upstate, but I go to school at Stony Brook. So, Jasmine, do you have a man?", I asked with a smile.

"Yea I do, but he isn't here right now. He lives in Syracuse."

Right away, that comment let me know that Shorty was definitely feeling me, and that she might not be a challenge at all. We kept on dancing for a couple more songs before exchanging phone numbers and agreeing to hook up later over the weekend. In my mind I was thinking more like hooking up tonight, but I wasn't going to force the issue and cause myself to look thirsty. Locating Abdul behind me I turned to him and said, "I'ma go check to see what the fellas are up to."

Without hesitation he agreed to accompany me, leaving the chick he was previously dancing with looking dumbfounded. When we located the fellas, they were sitting by the bar talking to a couple Hispanic dudes. I assumed they were good by the look of things and went back to doing me. Making my way back to the dance floor I turned to Abdul and asked "Did you get any digits yet?"

"Of course I did Bro, why wouldn't I?" Abdul replied with sheer confidence.

Right away I thought to myself amused, here we go again. Abdul is lying to kick it; ain't no one in their right mind gonna give him their phone number, unless they felt sorry for him. As I made it back to the dance floor, I felt a tap on my shoulder. Eager to find out who it was I turned around and was somewhat surprised to see my home-girl Michelle standing there looking sexy as hell in a lace crop top, blue low-rise jeans and a pair of all black Manalo's. Michelle and I attend the same college and had known each other for years prior to that.

With a smile on her face she asked "Do you wanna dance?"

Returning the smile, I replied, "Only because it's you."

For the past couple years Michelle and I have had a close-knit bond, and some way somehow whenever we were together we would always end up being intimate. While enjoying all the curves Michelle had to offer, I noticed Abdul cut in between a couple dancing, pulling the girl by the hand at the same time blatantly disrespecting her partner. At that very moment, I could sense there was about to be drama. Surprisingly, Shorty left the guy she was dancing with and started grinding all up on Abdul, which only made the other dude furious. He stared angrily at Abdul and at the same time tried to force himself on the chick. Out of nowhere, Abdul barked at him "Yo, are you a faggot or something?" The dude didn't even budge; he just stood there prolonging the staring match so I walked over to Abdul and asked if everything was aight. After realizing Abdul wasn't by himself and that he was out numbered, the dude turned around and walked away, feeling defeated.

"Good looking out, Drew. I swear, if that fool stood there staring a minute longer, I was going to break his face."

With a smirk on my face I replied, "No doubt, Bro, you know I got your back."

I then walked away momentarily, leaving Abdul to continue his grindfest with his dance partner, while I made my way back to Michelle to continue where we left off. The night was now coming to an end and I wanted to beat the crowd leaving the club, so I told Michelle I would give her a call later on when I got back to Long Island, after dropping off the guys. She nodded okay and whispered in my ear, "Try not to forget because I will be waiting for your phone call."

That gave me reassurance that I was getting some action tonight. I sure as hell didn't wanna go home and resort to Jergens lotion and online porn. The DJ started playing Usher's "Climax", as the lights came on signaling that the night was over. After leaving Michelle, I made a quick scan through the club locating Kendu and Clark sitting by the bar; and motioned them over so we could be on our way. Upon making it back to the car, a debate started on who got the most phone numbers over the course of the night and who was gonna getting laid. Out of nowhere Clark interrupted "Aye yo, I know this official spot where we could all get laid for the night and it's my treat."

I replied, "Yo my G, I wish I could. Don't get me wrong, that shit sounds really enticing, but not tonight. Maybe next time we could check it out."

I could tell that they weren't pleased by my response, but at the end of the day, I was driving so I had the final say in the matter. Sensing the awkwardness in the car Clark use the opportunity to change the topic and questioned, "Drew, did you notice we were by the bar all night?"

"Yeah, why, what's up?"

"Well I got a deal setup with the two dudes we were talking to for tomorrow. They're supposed to be selling us 10lbs of purple haze for $30,000, but instead of buying the weed, we're just going to meet them and take all they got. If you're trying to make some extra paper just let me know by midday tomorrow."

The offer was definitely tempting, but at the same time it appeared extremely risky and nothing like I have ever done before. I immediately calculated in my head 10lbs of haze meant that I would be getting at least 2lbs for myself. I knew dudes in Queens that hustled, so getting rid of it wouldn't be an issue. I could easily sell a pound for $4500, and I would even make a lot of more if I broke it down and sold nickel and dime bags.

"What would I have to do, and how safe is this?" I inquired trying to weigh the pros and cons, "I'm not tryna get caught."

"I'm only gonna need you to do the driving, and leave everything else up to us. You also don't have to worry about your license plate being exposed because I got one you could use instead and it's legit so the cops won't have any reason to mess with us. This should be like taking candy from a baby" Clark stated with a smirk on his face.

"Oh aight, I'm definitely gonna think about it and get back to you ASAP."

For the remainder of the ride back to Stony Brook, I was engulfed in my own world with thoughts of all the different possibilities and the money that could be made.

CHAPTER 3

Upon making it back to Long Island and dropping off the fellas, I was on my way home when Michelle ran across my mind, so I decided to give her a call to see if she was still up. On the third ring she answered "Hello" sounding sexy as ever.

"Hey babe what's good? It's me Drew."

"Oh hey Drew, where are you?"

"I'm on the road right now. I just got back from Brooklyn. What are you up to?"

"Nothing really, I just got out of the shower and was about to go check my emails and probably watch a movie after."

"Well, I was heading home so I wanted to check up on you to make sure you made it home safely." I was lying like a true pro, but shit everyone's got to lie at some point to get what they want.

"I thought you were coming over to see me." She stated with a hint of disappointment in her voice.

Yeah, I got her exactly where I want her, I thought to myself. "I figured it was too late, also that you might be too exhausted to have company."

"Nah, I'm actually fully awake"

"Alright then, I'm about to head over that way. Where are your housemates at?"

"They're probably sleeping by now. When you get here just give me a call and I'll come open the door for you. You can park in my spot; I parked up on the curb."

"OK, babe, I'll see you in a few."

After hanging up, I made a quick detour at the mobile gas station over on Main Street to pick up some condoms. To be honest, I really didn't like using them, especially when I was with Michelle. For some reason I just liked how it felt when we had intercourse without using a rubber, but I had to get them as a backup because sometimes she would front on me, telling me if I didn't have a condom I wasn't getting any. So I opted to be on the safe side by getting some. When I pulled up to her place, I parked and called her. She answered on the first ring, as if she was sitting around, eagerly anticipating my call.

"Hello Drew."

"Yeah, I'm outside."

"Okay, hold on, I'll be right there."

"Okay baby."

The second I made it on the porch, the front door swung open with Michelle standing in the middle of the doorway looking sexy as ever, wearing an oversized Polo T-shirt. I could tell she was bra-less because her nipples were looking extra perky through the T-shirt. She then took my hand and led me to her bedroom.

Entering the room, I noticed the lights were all off, giving way to the glare off the TV screen. Looking over to see what she was watching, I was a bit surprised; Michelle was in fact watching porn. I always knew she had a freaky side to her, but I would have never expected to find her watching smut. There was no telling what she was doing before I got there; but thought to myself. "Oh well, who am I to judge". Seeing that shit only turned me on more. I immediately turned to her with a smile saying "I see you got started without me, huh?"

With the most captivating smile she said "You're a fool, Drew."

That was the best form of an ice breaker, because immediately after she closed the door and gestured with her hand for me to come join her on the bed. As I sat on the bed, she walked right over and straddled me, placing her hands on my lower back, as my body tensed with anxiety. It was time to move in for the kill. Gently using my tongue to part her lips, I momentarily used my free hand to explore her body. Within seconds, I came to the realization that my intuition was in fact correct; she actually was completely naked beneath the T-shirt. Within seconds, my jeans were down to my knees with Michelle's head positioned between my legs as she made love to my dick. She was always the best when it came to giving head, and she always made sure to stay true to the title, HEAD MISTRESS. She was petite and sexy at 5ft 2inches with a caramel complexion; and weighed 110lbs with curves in all the right places. Not to mention she had a tongue ring, which made her head game even more exclusive. She had this thing she would do to spit all over my dick and then lick it all back up; as if it were the best tasting thing in the world. So, whenever she gave me head, I felt as if I was on cloud 9. As time elapsed we became completely naked, exploring each other, trying relentlessly to appease our sexual desires. In the middle of our foreplay session she stopped and asked, "Drew, do you have a condom?"

"Nah baby, that's my fault. I completely forgot to get some." I lied through my teeth, but if she gave me any flak, I would just have to go get them from my car.

"Damn Drew, you know how I feel about having sex without protection. I'm not trying to get pregnant."

"Don't worry about it baby. As I told you on numerous occasions, I know when to pull out."

Placing my tongue on her neck, I made small circular motions, gently sucking on her skin, tasting the sweet perspiration that secreted from her pores. With my free hand, I made my way down to her clit, massaging it mildly in hopes that she would let the issue slide and give in. It worked like a charm. Seconds later, her moans became uncontrollably louder. She sank her nails into my back signaling that what I was doing was working as planned. Panting and biting her bottom lip, she eased her head back before releasing her built up tension as she climaxed in ecstasy.

I couldn't resist the urge any longer, I needed to be inside her and I could tell by the look on her face that she wanted the same. Easing her way onto the bed, she placed her back against the sheets and pulled me on top of her whispering in my ear.

"I want you to fuck me Drew, fuck me."

Immediately after, she reached for my penis and eased it slowly inside her eagerly awaiting vagina. As all of my 10inches entered into her moistness, the sensation from her juices caused me to be on the verge of climaxing. I had to pace myself if I didn't want to be classified a minute man.

"Damn baby, your pussy feels oh so good." I exclaimed, thrusting all of me deep inside her tapping on the back of her vagina walls.

"It's all yours daddy, do as you please", she replied with a look of delight plastered on her face.

At that instant, I began pumping in and out, grinding my penis inside her trying relentlessly to find her g-spot. When I finally did, I made sure to keep my focus in that area, intensifying my strokes winding in a circular motion. We both became entranced, moving in unison as sweat trickled off our bodies. We went at it for a couple more hours, pleasuring each other into multiple orgasms until we passed out in each other's arms.

CHAPTER 4

I woke up the next morning admiring Michelle's beauty as
she laid there sleeping innocently. I definitely had some
strong feelings for her, but I've always told myself that's as
far as our relationship would go. Her friendship meant too
much for me to jeopardize it in anyway. Moments later I
got up, got dressed and was ready to leave. Before heading
out the bedroom, I heard sounds coming from outside the
kitchen area. I figured it had to be one of Michelle's
roommates out there, probably making breakfast or
something. Michelle had two roommates who also attended
the college, Lona and Shameka. All three of them were
banging, but Shameka was, without a doubt, the best
looking out of the crew. Last year, during the summer
break, I ended up sleeping with Lona. She wasn't a dime
piece, but whatever she lacked in the face department, she
more than made up for with her body. Over the summer
both Michelle and Shameka had gone back home for
vacation, while Lona remained in Stony Brook to take
summer courses. Because I had nowhere to stay for the
summer, Michelle gave me the option to crash in her
apartment; so, I jumped on the offer immediately. It was
way cheaper than having to rent somewhere. One night
after Lona and I returned from a house party all drunk and
wasted; we sat around flirting with each other, until one
thing led to another and we ended up having sex. I must
add that it was some of the wildest sex I've ever had.

Even after the summer vacation, we would still sneak
around and hook up with each other, but all in all, that was

our little secret. When I made my way out to the living room and looked towards the kitchen, the sight of Shameka, Michelle's other roommate, instantly put a smile on my face. She had on a closely fitted tank top and some gym shorts that snuggled so close to her ass, you would think they came 5 sizes too small. I've always been attracted to Shameka since the very first time I laid eyes on her, but I never had the opportunity to get with her. We would always flirt with each other, but that's as far as it went. Without a doubt, she had an official body and she generally used it to the best of her ability to get whatever she wanted. Every time I saw her, she reminded me of a darker version of Beyonce; to top it off, she had some sexy lips to compliment her body. The only thing that stopped me from going after her was her reputation of being a gold digger. Word on campus was that you had to spend major papers if you wanted to get with her, so that threw me off completely.

While heading for the front door she turned around smiling and said "Good morning Lance Armstrong."

Returning the smile, I asked, "Where did that come from?"

"I heard you and Michelle going at it last-night as if there was no tomorrow. Did you forget my room was right next to hers?"

"Well, the offer is always open to be the next contestant in my triathlon", I replied with a smirk on my face.

"Who knows, maybe one of these days I might have to take you up on that offer, because I feel like I might be getting a little too overweight."

"Well, you look good to me babes. But whenever you feel you might need the exercise, just holla at me."

"I most definitely will. Would you like to join us for breakfast?" She asked motioning towards the scrambled eggs and plantain she was currently making.

"That's okay, hun. I got some things I need to take care of, but thank you none the less."

"Ok sweetie, take care."

"You too."

When I made it outside to my car, I turned back on my Samsung Galaxy to check my messages. It was a regular thing for me to keep my phone off whenever I was with a female, just to avoid any possible bullshit.

When it came on, the screen notified me that I had three new voice mails. The first message was from my girlfriend Simone back in Albany calling to let me know that she loved me. Simone and I had been together for over a year now. We met through a mutual friend at a house party over in Canarsie, Brooklyn. When we first met, I knew then and there that she would be mines. I became captivated by her appearance immediately. She resembled Tyra Banks to the "T", she even had the forehead just like her. She was 5'8" tall, with a honey glazed, caramel complexion, long silky black hair, and weighed 120lbs with everything in the right proportion. We fell for each other instantly, and have been together ever since. When I pressed the button to hear the second message the recording said "Message two from phone number (917)255-4802, received at 3:15am" I was clueless as to who the message was from so I pressed 1 to listen to the recording.

"Hi Drew, this is Jasmine from the club. I was just calling to see If you made it home safe, and to let you know that I had fun last night. Give me a call whenever you get a chance. End of message."

"Message number three from, phone number (917)977-0367; received at 4:02am. Yo Drew, this is Clark, hit me back as soon as you get a chance, I got some good news. The dudes from the club called and said they are trying to do that as soon as possible, so get at me and let me know what's good. End of message". The first thing I did was to call Simone. It was now 7:30am, so I figured she would still be asleep, but I would just leave her a message letting her know I was okay. Just so she wouldn't be worried. Her phone rang four times before her voice-mail picked up.

"This is Simone, I am currently unavailable so please leave a message and I will get back to you as soon as possible; and if this is Drew, I just want you to know that I love you baby. To record a message please press 1, to send a text press 2." I pressed 1. "Please record now"; "Baby, I'm sorry I didn't receive your call last night; after the party I came home and went straight to bed because I had to get up early to go study at the library. I love and miss you. Talk to you soon, bye"

After hanging up, I was eager to call Jasmine to see if we could hook up later on, but I opted to call Clark instead; business before pleasure. When he answered the phone, we got right down to business.

"Yo Drew, what's good?"

"Ain't shit, you tell me?"

"Well, I spoke to the dudes from the club and we got everything set to go down tonight. We are we gonna to meet them at the Denny's off Main Street, and take that shit there; so, you down or what?"

"Yeah, Bro, I'm down with that. But before we go any further, how much money is there to be made and what will I have to do?"

"Well it's only going to be three of us, and dude is bringing 12lbs of that good good, so everyone is getting an even cut of 4lbs each; and the only thing I'll need you to do is drive."

"Aight bro, that sounds good to me. What time y'all plan on doing this?"

"Around 1 or 2am, so meet me at my place at 11 o'clock tonight and we will go over everything then."

"Aight no doubt, I'll holla at you later, one."

Upon making it off the phone, all kinds of thoughts began racing through my mind. What the hell am I getting myself into? What if something goes wrong and I get caught; what the hell would I say to my family? At the same time the thought of the money that could be made and the things I could do with the paper, immediately overshadowed everything else. They guaranteed it was risk free, so I was gonna take their word for it. When I made it home, I greeted my housemates, hopped in the shower and went straight to bed anxiously waiting what was ahead.

CHAPTER 5

I woke up at 8:30pm to the sound of my cellphone going off. Right away I knew who it was so I answered.

"Hey, what's up baby, how are you doing?"

"I'm doing ok. I've been trying to get in contact with you all day. Where the hell have you been?"

"My bad sweetie, I've been sleeping since earlier this morning when I left you that message. I told myself that I was only about to take a nap, but I was so exhausted from last night that I ended up passing out completely."

"Well, did you have fun?"

"Yeah, it was okay. I just needed to unwind a little."

"Where did you all go?" She inquired trying to catch me off guard.

"We went to a little club in Brooklyn."

"And how many chicken-heads did you give your number?"

"Only ten... nah I'm playing, baby. I love you too much to even think about playing you like that."

"You better, because I wouldn't want to have to go to jail for killing you and the bitch."

We both shared a laugh at that comment.

"Simone, you are too funny."

"Yeah, whatever you say. Well, baby, I'm about to go cook so I'll call you later on."

"Aight babes. I'll talk to you lata love."

She made a light chuckle and said "I love you more, baby" and hung up.

By the time I got off the phone it was already 9'o clock, so I had to get something to eat and get ready to go meet up with the fellas. I ended up leaving home at 10:50pm, so all in all, I was on schedule. When I made it to Clark's crib, Kendu was already there, and they were smoking and talking about what happened the night before.

"Yo, did anyone hear from Abdul since last night?" I asked.

Both Clark and Kendu erupted in laughter. Clark then stated, "Yo fam, that fool's been throwing up and shitting on himself since last night when you dropped him off." After hearing this I couldn't help but to laugh also. We goofed around for a lil bit before getting down to business, putting the plan together.

To my surprise, Kendu pulled out a 9mm, placing it on the couch right next to him and said, "Drew, we ain't got shit to worry about. If anyone of them dudes try anything funny, somebody getting laid the hell down."

"Ain't none of that happening; this should be as easy as one, two. Oh, and before I forget, here are the license plates to put on your car; they are legit so you don't need to worry about getting pulled over for fake plates.", Clark said.

We all came to a mutual agreement on the circumstances and how everything would go down, then sat patiently awaiting their phone call. Over an hour had elapsed before the phone rang; Ring, ring.

Clark wasted no time snatching the phone up on the second ring. "Hello, who dis?"

"'Sup Papi? This is Julio, the guy from earlier." stated a male in a Hispanic voice.

"Oh aight, what's good? Are we still on for tonight?"

"Yeah, we should be at the spot in 20 minutes."

"Aight cool, I'll meet you there."

I then motioned for Clark to find out the kind of car they would be in so it would be easier to spot them, so he asked "What's your car look like, so there won't be any problems spotting you."

"We'll be in a white 2010 Jeep Grand Cherokee. There's no way you could miss it."

"Okay then, I'll see you in a couple of minutes."

After Clark got off the phone, we double checked to make sure we had everything covered. Clark had some money to use as a front, just in case everything didn't go as planned. He had two bankrolls, one with a fifty-dollar bill on top and a hundred-dollar bills in the middle, while the other had a hundred-dollar bill on top and the same number of dollar bills rolled up inside to use as decoys. We then went outside and attached the replacement plates onto the car. As we got into the car, I told Kendu to stash the burner inside a compartment I had in the back seat leading all the way to the trunk. If we were to get pulled over it wouldn't be easily detected if searched. Moments later, I pulled away from the curb in my 2005 navy blue Nissan Maxima with both Kendu and Clark, up to no good, heading to Denny's to make some money. I must admit I felt kind a nervous as I'd never done anything like this before, and I was faced with the possibility that anything was liable to go wrong. But it was too late to turn back now. Throughout the entire ride, we all remained silent, consumed in our own thoughts, just bobbing our heads to the Notorious B.I.G. and Bone Thug's, 'Notorious Thugs'. Before pulling into the Denny's parking lot, I decided to drive by and circle the block just to make sure that Julio was already there. At first, I didn't spot their ride until Kendu pointed it out to me. After circling the block once more, I came back around and entered the parking lot, making sure to be cautious not to be seen by them. I opted to park all the way in the back, away from the Jeep. When we parked, Clark called Julio and informed him that we had arrived and asked if they wanted us to come to their car. Julio played right into our trap by saying it would be more convenient for us to come to him, so Clark agreed immediately.

After Clark gave us the 411, we started laughing saying "Yo son, we got this dude shook for real."

By now, Kendu had already snatched up the 9mm and was ready. I agreed to stay inside the car and keep the engine running with the lights off to make our get away much easier. "So, how will I know when to do what?" I asked.

Clark answered "If we not back within five minutes, something probably went wrong. So call my cell and if I don't pick up, just leave and we'll take it from there."

"Aight bro, I got you."

"But if you see us coming around the corner, just get ready to pull off."

As they got out the car headed to go meet with Julio, I sat in the car hoping and praying everything went as planned.

Two minutes went by and I began worrying, thinking that maybe this shit was too good to be true, and that this might all be a set up. Before the thought could even leave my mind, I saw Clark with two duffel bags in his hands, walking towards the car with Kendu not too far behind. My adrenaline started pumping immediately, and the minute they hopped into the car I sped off.

When we made it a block away, Clark opened the window and threw some items out of the car. I later found out that the items were in fact Julio and his friend's keys, cell-phones and wallets.

On the way back to Clark's crib, I made sure to cruise to the speed limit in an effort to not look suspicious.

CHAPTER 6

When we made it back to the apartment, we emptied the bags right away and began weighing the product to calculate our profits.

"Yo Clark, what the hell you took so long?", I asked.

He replied "When we got to the car this fool, Julio, was trying to front on us, telling me only one of us could get in and that the other had to wait outside."

Still filled with adrenaline Kendu exclaimed "Bro, as soon as I stepped into the car, I pulled out on them dudes and told them to keep their hands where I could see them; then my dog Clark hopped into the car and stripped them of everything and tied them up. So that's what caused the delay."

"Well I ain't gonna front, ya'll had me thinking they flipped the script and robbed ya'll instead" I said laughing.

By the time we got finished weighing the weed and counting out the money we had accumulated, everything came to 13lbs of weed and a total of $6,600 in cash. Apparently, they were about to give us an extra pound for free, but oh well, too bad we weren't intending on paying for it. After we got finished splitting up the proceeds of the nights endeavor, I ended up with 4lbs of weed and $2400. I was happy as hell. I had already made plans to sell 3lbs to my boy for $3200 a piece so I had a total of $9600 coming to me, and all in a couple minutes work. I felt as if I could really get used to this.

Before splitting up, we agreed to hook up tomorrow night to go celebrate. On the drive back to my apartment, I called up my boy D and told him I had what he needed, and agreed to stop by to drop it off. Upon arrival at his apartment, I called him to come meet me outside.

As he entered the car, I saw he had a big smile plastered on his face so I asked, "What's good bro?"

"Ain't shit right now. Did you get that for me?", he replied.

"Yeah, you got ma money?" I asked with a light chuckle.

"Of course. Why, you wanna check to make sure it's all there?"

"Nah, I'm all good. I've known you long enough to know that you wouldn't snake me", I replied. I didn't know D to be a snake, he was a stand-up dude and a straight up gangster.

"Well, just because you said that, I'm not going to weigh the weed," he stated with his eyebrows slightly raised smiling. His comment caused us both to erupt in laughter. Ever since I met D, I took a liking to him and respected him to the fullest. I've known him for a little over a year now. We ended up meeting through a mutual friend, and ever since we became really close. As he turned to face me I could see a serious yet concerned look on D's face, "Yo Drew, what you're doing is nothing to be played with, so make sure you know exactly what you're getting yourself into. You've come too far in achieving your goals in life to fuck around and get knocked on some bullshit. You know that if you ever need anything, I got you."

"Good looking out, D. I got love for you too. I promise I 'ma just mess with this a few more times and that's it; I'm just trying to accumulate enough money to trade in my Nissan and get that new 2015 Cadillac Escalade."

"Whatever you say, if you ever need me for anything, you know how to get in contact with me."

"Aight bro, good looking out."

We embraced each other, then did our sequenced handshake. After making his way out the car, I pulled away from the curb heading home in deep thought. I had always looked up to D as a mentor. He had accomplished so much by acquiring his Masters in Business Management, owning his own company and at the same time maintaining his street credibility as one of the most ruthless drug dealers in New York City. I went straight home to drop everything off and to figure out my next move for the night. I was in no way trying to be caught riding dirty by these racist ass cops. By the time I made it home, all my housemates had already left except Jermaine. Maine and I had known each other since our days of playing High School soccer for two rival schools in Amherst. Every time our teams played each other, a fight always ensued. Maine was more of laid-back type of dude and similar to me in more ways than one, so we got along great. When I got to my room, I called Maine inside and told him about what had gone down and showed him the profit I made. He took interest immediately and asked me if I could put him on. I told him it wasn't a guarantee, but that I would have to get back to him on it.

"What do you have planned for the night?" I asked.

He replied, "Nothing. I'm just here bullshitting. Why, do you have something in mind?"

"I was thinking about calling up this chick I met last night to see what's good. I'll make sure to see if she got a home girl or something for you."

"Aight, that's what's up, just holla at me and let me know what the deal is."

I waited for him to make his exit before I got up and closed the door. Making my way over to the closet, I stashed the weed and money inside my dirty clothes hamper.

Grabbing my phone, I decided to give my baby Simone a call, just to ensure she wouldn't be worried or stressing me thinking I'm cheating on her in any way.

After getting off the phone with Simone I called Jasmine immediately after. She didn't answer so I left her a message letting her know that I had called.

It was almost 2am, so I figured she would be asleep by now but I felt it was definitely worth the try.

Not even a minute after I hung up, my phone started ringing. The number showed up as being unknown so I figured it was Simone playing games, messing with me, so I answered.

"Hello, who dis?"

"Hi Drew, it's me Jasmine, did you try calling me just now?"

"Yes, I did. My bad for calling you this late. You ran across my mind so I just wanted to see what you were up to."

"Oh, okay. Well, I was just chilling in bed, doing some studying. "

"I'll take it that you're in for the rest of the night then."

"Not necessarily. What are you getting into?"

"I was trying to get up with you to watch a movie or something, Netflix and chill" I replied with a smirk, hoping she would agree.

"Well, a break from all this work doesn't sound that bad after all."

"So, are you accepting my offer?"

"I guess I might. I just hope your girl is not a psycho or nothing."

"Who the hell lied to you that I got a girl?" I asked, hoping she didn't somehow know too much about me already.

We both laughed at my comment, giving way to a sigh of relief on my end.

"I just hope your man doesn't catch you coming over here and try shooting up my place because I haven't installed the bullet proof windows as yet

She made a light chuckle then said "You ain't got to worry about that. He's 8hrs away from here."

"Yeah, okay. Well, I guess I could relax a bit now", I replied, causing us both to share a laugh.

"Hey Drew, do you smoke trees?"

"Yeah, I do."

"Do you have any, or do you need me to pick some up?"

"Nah, I got that covered. Oh, and Jasmine, where are your home girls at?

"They all went back out to that club in Brooklyn."

"Oh cool. I was asking because my housemate is here with me and I didn't want him feeling left out."

"Well, we could all chill together. It's not a problem."

Immediately, I thought to myself, "this chick might just be a straight freak. Before getting off the phone, I gave her the address and hung up. Shortly after, I went and told Maine what the deal was.

"Bro, whatever is clever. If Shorty getting down like that, it's nothing. You acting like this would be the first time we're sharing a chick." he exclaimed laughing.

"Maine, you're a fool fa real" I replied with a smirk on my face.

Thirty minutes had already passed before Jasmine called, letting me know that she was already on my block and to look out for her. When I went out onto the porch, I saw her pulling up to the curb.

"I'm a definitely have some fun tonight." I thought to myself as she got out of the car, her attire caught my attention immediately. She was wearing a powder blue Juicy Couture sweat suit that fit so tight, it appeared to be painted on to her body. We greeted each other with a close embrace. I firmly cupped her ass cheeks, getting a sneak preview of what was in store. When we went into my bedroom, Maine was already there rolling up three blunts, so I introduced them right away.

"Hey Jasmine, this is my housemate, Maine."

"'Sup, Jasmine? Nice to meet you", Maine replied with open arms.

She replied, "Same here, Maine", as they embraced each other.

Making her over to me she asked, "So Drew, what's your movie selection like?"

"Well, right now you only got two options: 'Friday' and 'Half Baked'. Which one would you like to see?"

"I'm a let you to choose."

"Aight then, I'm a pop in 'Half Baked'. That shit is hilarious!"

Seconds later, Maine lit the three blunts and passed them around so we each had our own individual blunt. He then went and sat in the recliner, while Jasmine sat in bed next to me. I had to do something to break the ice, so I leaned over and whispered in her ear; "Did you check your rear-view mirror to make sure you weren't being followed?"

She burst out laughing and said, "I thought I saw a female trailing me. Maybe that was one of your hoes or something."

"Yeah, yeah, whatever you say" I stated with a smile.

Placing my left hand on her thighs, I began making soft, wet kisses on her neck while I fondled her breast through her top with my free hand. This had her moaning like crazy, edging me on to continue doing what I did best. Next thing I knew, she had my dick in her hands stroking and massaging it. Easing her way off the bed she urged me to pull my pants down. She didn't need to tell me this twice. My hands began moving with urgency as she stripped butt-naked. Maine was still chillin in the recliner smiling from ear to ear undoubtedly pleased with how things were going down. Jasmine's body was nothing less than banging and seeing her standing there in front of me fully nude caused my manhood to stand at full attention. Sexual tension encompassed the room and our inhibitions were no longer bottled up. Seconds later, she leaned over, placing her lips on my dick as she kissed it ever so gently; taking it into her mouth inch by inch. Soon, she had all 10 inches inside her mouth, deep-throating it like a true pro.

Seeing this as the most opportune time, Maine made his way behind her and gently kissed Jasmine's clit while fingering her honeycomb. She didn't put up any form of resistance, which urged Maine on even more, intensifying his excitement as he focused on pleasuring her orally.

Maine was known as the pussy monster due to his love of eating pussy, so Jasmine was definitely in great hands. The sensation from getting her clit licked and sucked rippled throughout her body, causing her to gag all over my chocolate bar. We remained in that position for a couple of minutes until the tip of my dick began to tingle, signaling an orgasm was on the way. Jasmine could tell I was on the verge of climaxing by the look on my face. Looking up at me she eased my dick out her mouth for a split second, urging me to cum in her mouth. She didn't have to tell me that twice. Moments later I felt a vibration in my hips, indicating that I was close to exploding, so I placed my hands on her head, forcing it downward onto my dick as I erupted inside her mouth. The night was definitely building up to be one to remember. We were all entranced in the most intense sexual experience ever, fulfilling our wildest desires and undoubtedly satisfying Jasmine completely. By the time we got done, it was going on 5'o clock in the morning. Ironically, I thought to myself, "I wouldn't want to be Jasmine's man. If Simone ever did some shit this grimy and I found out, I would probably end up killing her and whoever she was fucking." But at the moment, it wasn't fair to be judging Jasmine at all. After she got dressed and ready to leave I accompanied her to the car and told her to give me a call when she got home.

She had the nerve to turn around and say, "I really hope you don't look at me differently after tonight."

"Nah, of course not. Why would I? It was all clean fun babes," I replied, lying my ass off. I had no intentions whatsoever of calling her again, even though it was fun. I tried my best not to get too carried away at times. She then hopped into her car with a smile plastered on her face and waved goodbye. As she pulled off, I went right inside to Maine's room to go talk to him, but upon making my way into the room, I realized this fool was passed out on his bed snoring. I decided to get some rest myself. I was too exhausted to sit up and wait for Jasmine's call.

CHAPTER 7

Later that afternoon, I woke up to the sounds of music coming from my living room. Right away, I knew it had to be Maine out there acting a fool. I soon made it out of bed and went to the bathroom to brush my teeth and wash my face before I did anything else. As I went into the living room, all three of my housemates were there messing around as usual. Altogether, I had the best housemates you could ever wish for. We all got along well because our personalities were so much alike. We ended up meeting last year on campus while living in the same dormitory, and we hit it off immediately. After spending a semester on campus, we all agreed that the dorms were for lames, so we decided to get an apartment and we've been rooming together ever since.

As soon as Maine saw me he smiled and said "There is the man of the hour," causing everyone else to laugh.

 I replied, "Yo whatever. You were the one acting like Mr. Marcus, not me."

Mr. Marcus was a popular black porn star that made a name for himself with his oral techniques.

"Drew, tell these fools what really went down last night to prove that I'm not lying; and let them know how sexy home girl was."

"Yo, all I got to say is that both of you missed out on something real special, but don't worry Maine and I had both you' all shares, and then some."

"Drew, you are a retard for real." Maine said laughing.

"So, Omar, how was the party last night, and how many numbers did y'all get, if any?" I inquired.

He replied, "I don't know why you keep on thinking I don't get busy in the club, because I most definitely do. In fact, ask Chris what happened last night and who was all up on me for most of the night, ready to give me some nookie."

"Yo, Chris, what's this clown talking about?"

"He probably talking about Sheane. I don't know about the giving him some part, but she was definitely all up on him last night. As a matter a fact, she did say to tell you hi."

Sheane and I were seeing each other last semester. Our relationship was going good until Simone decided to pay me a surprise visit one weekend. This ended up forcing me to come clean with Sheane after she came over to my place to see me and Simone answered the door. I had to give her props though, because she could have easily spilled her guts and told on me, but she didn't, and that's why I still have love and respect for her. Ever since then, she has carried a lot of hatred for me and from time to time she would do little things in an effort to hurt me. So that stunt she pulled last night didn't come as a surprise to me, not one bit.

"Yo O, you hear me, I ain't even worried about Shorty. She's still stuck on what happened between us in the past and is steady trying to get me back. If you really want to, you can go ahead and see what's up with her. I honestly wouldn't care."

He smiled after my comment and said, "Drew, you know I couldn't do no shit like that."

In my mind, I thought, "Yeah whatever. If the opportunity ever presented itself, he would jump on it immediately".

That topic was going nowhere so I asked, "What do ya'll have planned for the day?"

Chris answered "Nothing. Why, what's up?"

"I was thinking about going to the gym on campus to play some ball. It's been a while since I schooled y'all."

They all answered "Yeah, whatever. Let's go then."

"Aight, bet".

Soon after, we all got ready and were heading to the Alumni Arena. I made sure to remind Maine to bring his camcorder so that we would have everything recorded. This was a regular thing for us to tape our games so whenever we got back to the house we could watch it and make fun each other. Upon arriving at the gym, we headed straight for the basketball court. We played two on two, best out of three, game eleven. It was Chris and O, against Maine and I. Maine was 6 feet tall and weighed around 190lbs; he was a beast on the court as he had both speed and agility. Both

O and Chris played football so they were relatively big in body. Whenever we played against each other they would always try to use their body to post us up, but with Maine's and my quickness combined, it was hard for them to contain us. They ended up whipping our asses the first game 11-7. The second game went by quick. I kept on hitting jumper after jumper, while Maine abused Chris in the post, helping us to win the game 11-5. The third game was the hardest; no one wanted to lose so everyone played their best trying to gain bragging rights. At one point, my team fell behind 10-6, until Maine made four straight baskets to tie the game at 10-10. We were all exhausted so we decided the game would be straight eleven, instead of prolonging it. Snatching the ball off the floor, I threw it at O yelling, "Checkup, bum!" He then rolled it towards Maine with a smirk on his face as he got into the defensive stance. As Maine passed me the ball, Chris came running up to me with his arms out, swiping at the ball to no avail. I then dribbled the ball to my right, next crossing over to my left. When Maine saw me coming his way, he immediately set a pick for me causing Chris to bump into him as I pulled up and shot the ball. Swoosh, all net. I immediately started yelling, "Game over, you bums!"

Both Maine and I slapped high fives while we kept on talking shit. Turning to Chris I said, "Y'all dudes are trash, don't you dare call us out again. Ay yo Maine, make sure you got that shot on tape dude, I might need it at my Hall of Fame inauguration." We both kept on laughing as we made our way to the locker room.

On the way home, we made sure to stop to get something to eat at a Jamaican restaurant over on Main St. I was starving to death and so were the fellas. By the time we got home, I rolled a couple blunts giving everyone their own while we sat around watching the game off the camcorder, cracking jokes.

"Yo, I'll be right back fellas", I stated getting up heading towards my bedroom.

It was getting dark outside so I called up Clark to see if we were still on for the night.

He answered on the third ring, "What's good, homie?"

I replied "Ain't shit right now. What's the deal with you?"

"I'm over here, chilling with Abdul."

"Oh aight. Tell him I said what up. Before I forget, are we still up for later?"

"Yeah, but we might have to hit up at a different spot."

"Why, what's wrong with the one in Brooklyn?"

"Well, since last night, them dudes we robbed been calling my phone leaving threatening messages."

"Bro, they just mad they got hit up, that's all."

"Well the phone number they had was for a burner anyways, so I threw that shit away," Clark stated.

"So, you got nothing else in mind?"

"Well, we could check out this strip club up in the South Bronx. I heard that shit be jumping and the dancers there are sexy as hell."

"That sounds good to me. Then we could try that spot you told me about with them prostitutes."

"Drew, I didn't know you were a freak like that" he stated laughing.

"Nah bro, I just feel like having some fun tonight, that's all."

"Aight, if you say so. Before I forget, did you manage to get rid of that merchandise from last night?"

"Yeah, I'm almost out. Well, I'll be over to pick you all up at around 11 o'clock, so be ready."

"Aight my dude, peace."

When I got off the phone with Clark, I called up Simone to let her know my plans for the night because I wasn't trying to hear no bullshit later on. At first, she was trying to persuade me not to go until I reassured her that it was all about her and no one else. With that said she dropped the issue and told me to make sure I called her in the morning. For some reason, I felt as if I was let off the hook too easily, which only caused me to think that she actually might have plans of her own for the night. Often it would cross my mind that she was probably cheating on me with some other guy and that her guilty conscience might be eating her up which was why she acted the way she did at times, but then again, I could be wrong.

Soon afterward, I headed back to the living room to go chill with my housemates. We sat around playing video games and acting a fool for a couple more hours until I got up to get ready. I had already made up my mind that I was going to go all out tonight, stunting like I was that dude.

As I made my way out the shower, I went straight to the closet to pick out what I was wearing. I decided to throw on a brown and black Gucci outfit with the jacket to match, and a fresh pair of all white Air Force ones I picked up last week. I even went as far as to throw on my jewelry, something I didn't like doing too much because that usually attracted the wrong crowd, but tonight I really didn't give a damn because I was BALLING....I ended up putting on my 2 1/2 ct. diamond bracelet with the matching pinky ring, and my black Michael Kors diamond bezel watch, all of which I have received from Michelle over the years as gifts.That was one thing I could say about Shorty. She was definitely not stingy with her paper, especially if she had love for you. Before I left out the door I grabbed my wallet and $2000 out my stash for spending money. Tonight, I was definitely gonna party like a true playa should.

CHAPTER 8

When I got to Clark's place, I called to notify him that I was downstairs and within seconds they were outside heading towards the car. Both Kendu and Abdul went straight for the back seat while Clark sat in the front with me. I wasted no time picking at Abdul as I turned to him with a smirk and asked "What the hell happened to you yesterday bro? I heard you had the double whammy. You had shit coming out your mouth and ass at the same time."

We all erupted in laughter as Abdul sat there looking dumbfounded. He replied "Yo son, I think that dude I was beefing with the other night put some kind of voodoo shit on me. That's my word; he looked Haitian anyways. I swear that if I see that fool ever again, I'ma end up whipping his ass."

"Aight Rambo, just make sure you don't end up getting your ass whipped", I replied laughing my ass off, causing everyone else to join in, laughing at him.

"Ay yo Kendu, roll something up for the road", I stated before pulling off.

On the way to the strip club we kept on smoking and cracking jokes on each other just to pass the time. A couple of miles before we got to the Bronx, we made sure to put out the smoke and to air the car out with some air freshener. I wasn't tryna get pulled over and arrested for no bullshit so I asked everyone if they had their IDs on them. Everyone replied yes, so we were good to go thus far.

By the time we pulled up to the strip club, everyone was hyped. When we made it to the entrance there were two bad, Hispanic strippers dressed in some extra sexy negligee. We paid $10.00 a piece to get in and were given members only applications to fill out; shit, we definitely had plans on becoming regulars. Inside the club was filled with gorgeous women everywhere — some half-naked and some in their birthday suits — walking around nonchalantly. Right away I thought to myself, "Yessss, I'm in female heaven"

The place was jam packed with patrons everywhere so it was relatively hard for us to find a table. Luckily, we ended up finding one directly in front the main stage. On stage were two exotic black females performing a lesbian show that had everyone in the audience in a frenzy throwing money at them egging them on to continue. Meanwhile, a waitress walked over to our table to take our orders. Her body caught my attention immediately. She had on some black short shorts and a white crop top that exposed her navel piercing, which only enhanced her sex appeal.

With a pleasant smile on her face she asked, "What can I get you guys?"

I was thinking about asking for her phone number, but opted not to because I wasn't trying to be the laughingstock of the night if I was turned down. I decided to do a little bit more to show her I was that dude by ordering drinks for everyone.

"Could we please get two bottles of Crystal on ice with four glasses?"

She replied, "No problem, sir. That will be $340.00."

I slowly pulled out a couple hundred-dollar bills, making sure to flash my wad of cash so that she could see it as I peeled off $360 and told her to keep the change.

"Thank you very much sir. I'll be right back with your drinks.", she said smiling seductively. After she left I turned to the fellas and told them, "Yo, watch the response of these females after this. I bet you all $50 a piece that within the next minute or so this table is going to be packed with strippers.

They all replied "Bet is on, son."

Meanwhile, on stage, the freak show was still going on. One of the females was now sitting on top of the other's face while she penetrated her with a dildo the size of baseball bat. When the waitress finally made it back to our table, she had a wide smile on her face as she stared directly at me. Placing our order on the table, she turned to me and said, "If you guys need anything at all I'll be right over by the bar. Oh, and by the way, my name is Candy."

We all shook our heads and replied "Thank you."

I don't know what the others were thinking, but I was trying to figure out just how sweet Candy actually was. Just as I had predicted, within seconds, three gorgeous strippers made their way over to our table, flirting and trying to get us to go to the V.I.P. with them. At this point, the freak show on stage had ended and the dancers had just got finished picking up their money before they went backstage to freshen up.

Over the speakers the DJ announced, "And now, for the main event, I present to you the lovely and seductive Eve."

As Eve made her way onto the stage, I became captivated by her beauty instantly. She gave full meaning to the word beautiful. She had long, black, silky hair that flowed down to the middle of her back. She was only about 5 ft. 3 inches tall, but with the Alexander McQueen's she had on she looked to be about 5'7", with milky chocolate complexion and weighed about 115lbs, with a banging body. Right away, I thought to myself, "That's who I'm a get with tonight." When I turned around, I saw both Kendu and Clark heading towards the V.I.P section with two strippers, while Abdul sat at the table conversing with his lady friend. She was also cute, but she just wasn't my type. Right now, I had my focus solely on one person, and that was Eve.

R Kelly's hit, 'Feelin' on Yo Booty' was blaring through the speakers, which seemed to inspire Eve as she started her performance. Her movements were precise and sensual as she stripped her body of the negligee she had on piece by piece. Watching her, I became completely mesmerized. I began pulling money out of my pocket and throwing it at her, not giving a damn who saw me and what they thought. In my mind, this woman was worth all that and then some. Tapping me on my shoulder Abdul said "Yo Drew, I'm about to head to the V.I.P lounge with Shorty. I think she is about to give me some a that good good."

"Aight son, do you, and make sure she doesn't get you for all your money", I replied smiling.

When I redirected my attention back to the stage, Eve was already topless, exposing her beautiful and perky breasts. She then made her way over to my section, stopping directly in front my table. She began staring at me as she motioned me closer with her hands. Making my way over to her, my instincts told me that I had her where I wanted her. When I got to the stage she got on all fours positioning her ass in my face as she clapped her cheeks repeatedly, causing me to become aroused and at the same time yearning for more. I immediately reached into my pants pocket, pulling out a $20 bill and placing it directly between her thong. After doing this, she turned around planting a kiss on my cheek, smiling and said, "Thank you."

I returned the smile and whispered in her ear, "I would really like to see you later on."

That comment put a smile on her face as she walked away, collecting her money that was on stage before she making her exit. For the next couple minutes, I sat at the table drinking and thinking about Eve and how intoxicated I was by her. I was jarred from my thoughts by a tap on my back. Even before I turned around, my instincts told me who it was. The Chanel perfume she had on gave her away immediately. I turned around saying, "It's a pleasure to see that you took me up on that offer."

"How could I possibly say no to such a charming and sexy man?" she asked with a pleasant smile.

As she eased into the chair next to me, she made sure to keep eye contact the entire time. I was definitely feeling her style and I could tell that she was feeling me also. Looking at her sitting next to me, I absorbed her absolute beauty. Halle Berry and J-Lo ain't got nothing on her.

"Eve, would you like something to drink?" I asked gently licking my lips.

"Yes, I'll have a glass of Grey Goose, thank you."

I then motioned Candy over to take our orders.

"Hey Candy, I'd like to order a bottle of Grey Goose on ice please, with two wine glasses."

"OK sir, one bottle of Grey Goose coming right up."

As she walked away to get our drinks, I turned to Eve and asked, "So what's a beautiful woman like you doing in a place like this?"

"I just do this every once in a while, to make some extra paper, and to occupy my time", she replied. "Does your girl know you're here at a strip club?"

I replied, "Well, I'm single at the moment. And I'm assuming the same goes for you, because your man would have to be crazy to allow you to work here."

She made a light chuckle then said "Well, I don't have a man, for your information; and you're right about the second part. I hear it all the time."

Candy had now made her way back to our table with our drinks, so I told her thanks and made sure to give her a $20 tip, which had her smiling. I was probably one of the best customers she'd had in a while.

After pouring us both glasses of Grey Goose, I turned to Eve and asked, "Well, where are you from, beautiful?"

"I'm actually from California, but I've been living out here for the past couple years with my brother. What about you, what's your name, if you don't mind me asking?"

I thought to myself, "Your wish is my command". This situation was kind of ironic because I would always make fun of my boys, clowning them and calling them suckers for love. Yet, here I was, falling head over heels for a stripper I'd only known for a few minutes.

"Nah, it's not a problem. All my friends call me Drew, and I'm actually from Upstate New York", I replied, making sure to stress on the New York.

"Well Drew, you could call me Evelyn or Eve, it's your choice. What do you say we go to the V.I.P lounge? I just might have a surprise for you back there."

"How can I turn down an offer so promising?" I asked smiling. "Also, just out of curiosity, what is your nationality?"

"Well, I am Cuban and Dominican," she replied as we got up from our table heading towards the V.I.P. section.

When we made it to the V.I.P, I reached into my pockets for some money to pay her, but she stopped me and said, "There's no need for that. I told you I had a surprise for you and I always stay true to my promise. Just sit back, relax and enjoy."

I looked at the couch behind me and was skeptical about sitting on it because it looked kinda dingy, and there was no telling what was on it, but at the moment I was left with no other options. Mystical's 'Shake it Fast', began blazing through the speakers as Eve positioned herself on top of me, grinding really slow and hard, causing my manhood to rise to its full potential. "Drew, you can touch me if you want to. I promise I won't bite… unless you want me to", she purred in a sexy tone. She didn't have to tell me twice. I started fondling her breasts, taking my time to massage them with care. Soon afterward, she began grinding on me even harder, moaning as she leaned over slipping her tongue inside my ear. I wasted no time following suit, as I placed my hands between her legs, slowly pushing her thong to the side while playing with her clit. Her panties were now drenched with her juices as she leaned towards me, sucking on my neck, leaving traces of saliva as she made her way to my chest.

Stopping momentarily, she asked, "Do you have a condom?"

" Yes", I replied eagerly pulling it out my jacket pocket, anticipating what was about to happen next.

Easing her way up off me, she unbuckled my pants pulling it all the way down to my knees. Then reached inside my boxer shorts and pulled out my dick. I could tell by the expression on her face that she was, in fact pleased with what she saw. She wasted no time opening her mouth, giving way for my love muscle to enter. After a couple minutes of her pleasuring me orally, I felt as if I was about to orgasm. At that point, I stopped her for a minute so I could put the condom on. After slipping on the rubber, I picked her up placing her on her back on the couch. She instantly spread her legs eagerly for me, exposing her clean-shaved vagina. I proceeded to ease my chocolate bar inside her warmth, inch by inch, causing her facial expression to change as she writhed in sheer ecstasy.

Staring into my eyes she said, "I want you to make me cum, Papi", moving her hips in a circular motion, increasing the heavenly sensation we were both experiencing. I was determined to make a lasting impression, so I reciprocated her movements, applying just the right amount of pressure. We became so engulfed in each other that we completely lost track of time. An hour had already gone by and we were still going at it. Seconds later, one of the bouncers came knocking on our booth saying, "Yo Eve, you're on in 15 minutes".

"Thanks a lot, John", she muttered as she lay on her back with me positioned between her legs.

Right away, I increased my pace, determined to make her climax before she had to leave me. It didn't take me long to reach my goal as she began panting and moaning loudly, indicating that she was coming. Her legs began shaking uncontrollably as she covered her mouth, trying to suppress the sounds of ecstasy. Apparently, she needed some reinforcement because her hands didn't do much to contain her voice as she yelled, "I'mmmmmmmmm cummmmmmminnggg."

The way she sank her nails in my back and bit her bottom lip, I could tell she was satisfied with our little encounter, and so was I. After we both got dressed she turned to me and said, "Thank you for a wonderful experience, Drew".

"No. Thank you. I wish we had enough time for me to show you the reason I got my nickname.", I replied with a smile plastered on my face.

"And what might that be?" she asked interestedly.

"Stallion", I replied.

That comment put a smile on her face, "Why don't you wait for me until the club closes, then we could go back to my place to finish where we left off."

Her offer was definitely enticing, but I couldn't play the fellas like that, leaving them stranded all because of Shorty, knowing damn well I'm their only way home.

"Damn baby, I honestly wish I could, but I came here with a couple friends and I am their only ride home."

"Too bad, Drew. I would've definitely made it worth your while."

"That's messed up Ma, you ain't gotta rub it in my face like that.", I stated with a frown teasing her.

"OK then, how about we exchange phone numbers so we can hook up some other time, because I am definitely trying to find out how you got that nickname" she said smiling.

After exchanging phone numbers, we embraced and promised to hook up again real soon.

When I made my way back to our table, both Kendu and Clark were sitting there grinning from ear to ear, so I asked, "What the hell is so funny?"

They both replied, "You, big daddy."

"Both of you are clowns", I said, smiling to myself and relishing in what just went down.

"Where is Abdul at?" I asked.

"That fool is in the bathroom, throwing up all over himself," Kendu replied. "While he was in the back, getting a lap dance from this fine-looking stripper, this fool fucks around and throws up all over the chick. I'm surprised you didn't hear the commotion back there. Then again, I can see why, you being all up in some pussy and shit. That shit was hilarious though, just about the entire club was back there having a good laugh at Abdul's expense."

"Oh word, did you all check up on him to make sure he is alright in the bathroom?"

Before either of them had a chance to answer, I spotted Abdul exiting the bathroom heading over towards us.

When he made it over, I could tell he was embarrassed by the stupid look on his face.

He turned to me and asked, "Yo Drew, are you ready to leave? I feel like shit right now."

I couldn't help myself, I just had to add fuel to the fire so I said "And you look and smell like shit too. Yo Clark, check his drawers for me, he might have some shit still in them."

We all burst out laughing at that.

"Let's get out of here. I'm exhausted anyways; this has been a long night."

On the ride back, everyone had passed out completely leaving me all to myself, so I threw in Bob Marley's greatest hits into my CD changer and zoned out to the words of each song as they played. Thoughts of the future began running through my mind. Thoughts of where I would be in the next couple of months. Would I be dead, alive, or somewhere in prison, lost in the system? I knew for a fact that if I continued to get involved in these drug deals, at any time things could go wrong. That night, I made a promise to myself that I would focus more on getting my shit together, getting my degree, and making myself and my loved ones proud.

CHAPTER 9

Within the next couple of weeks everything went as planned. I ended up passing all my mid-terms accumulating three A's, and two B's and I was also $7000 closer to copping my Cadillac truck. I had also been dedicating a lot of my time to chilling with Eve and at the same time I was avoiding Simone, which caused our relationship to deteriorate. I had very strong feelings for Simone, but right now those feelings were being overshadowed by the feelings I had developed for Eve. Wherever either of us was, it was a guarantee you would spot the other. We were just inseparable, and our sex life was nothing but terrific, which was the icing on the cake. Whatever chance we got, we were all over each other.

In bed one night after making love, we sparked up a conversation about our families and what life was like growing up. I figured it was the right time, especially if we had plans on taking our relationship to the next level. "So, Drew what's up with your parents? You don't ever talk about them." Eve asked while she sat up in bed.

"Well, I figured you would not be that interested in learning about my family."

"Why would you say that, Drew? Of course I want to know about your family, and hopefully I could get to meet them some day."

"Well, you don't ever talk about your family. The only thing I know is that you stay with your brother in New Rochelle."

"Okay, how about we get all that out of the way right now, and get to know each other a little better."

"Fair enough hun. Well both my parents are in the legal field. My mom is a paralegal and my father is a corporate lawyer" I stated.

"Oh that's cool baby, I'm assuming you must have been spoiled growing up."

"Nah not really, my younger sister Rose is the spoiled one; I try to be independent and go for mines, without much help from my parents. Don't get me wrong, they are some of the most pleasant and loving people you could ever meet, and they sure as hell worked hard to get to where they are today. So, what about your folks?" I sensed a bit of hesitation when I asked, but she proceeded to answer nonetheless.

"I hope you don't look at me differently after I tell you this, but my family is the complete opposite of yours."

"What do you mean by that?" I asked with concern.

"Well my father is one of the biggest drug dealers in the Dominican Republic, but he is a wonderful individual and so is my mother. They have been together for the past 30 years, and I am the younger of two kids. My older brother Eric controls most of the drug trade from Canada to the U.S. coming in through Niagara Falls."

I was completely speechless as I sat there looking at her trying to register what I was hearing. She then went on to say, "Drew, I would love for you to meet my brother. I have a feeling you two would get along perfectly."

Right away my criminal instincts started kicking in, so I asked "Do you think he would mind fronting or selling me some work?"

She was kind a hesitant with her response as she said, "I don't know Drew, I honestly wouldn't want to see you getting caught up in that type of lifestyle. You've got too much going for you right now to want to jeopardize it like that."

I thought to myself, "if she only knew the half of what's been going on, she wouldn't be saying that". I decided to go along with the charade, just so I wouldn't taint the image she had of me. So I replied, "Baby, I'm not trying to make a living doing this, all I'm trying to do is make enough money to help out with my tuition and save up enough money to buy a truck."

"Drew, if you need anything, all you have to do is let me know and I'll gladly give it to you."

"Baby, I don't want to take your money, it just wouldn't feel right. I promise you, I won't get caught up in the bullshit. All I need is probably a couple months to stack some money, and then I'm done."

"I just don't want to lose you babe, but if that's what you want, I'll try and set up a meeting with y'all on Friday.

He's always at the club on Fridays so that shouldn't in any way interfere with his schedule."

"Thanks a lot baby," I replied as I leaned towards her, planting a kiss on her neck.

As my hands began exploring her body she whispered in my ear, "Drew, I think I'm falling for you. Just promise me you won't ever leave me or break my heart."

"I promise baby, I will never hurt you."

That night we made love for what felt like an eternity. I was without a doubt in love with Eve and wanted what we had to last. I just hoped deep down that nothing would come between us and that I wasn't making a bad decision.

The following morning, I woke up to a note on the pillow lying next to me. Realizing it was from Eve, I picked it up and it read.

'Hey baby I know you probably woke up expecting to see me so I apologize for leaving so soon. I had to head back to take care of something for my brother. I also got some good news; he agreed to meet with you on Friday at 10pm, so when we talk I'll let you know more. Oh and Drew, thanks a lot for last night.

Love Eve.'

After I read the note I sat up in bed thinking "Drew, you better know what you are getting yourself into, because if this thing happens to backfire on you, it would not be pretty.

I had to prepare for Friday, just in case everything went as planned, so I called up the one person I knew I could depend on in this type of situation, my main man D. He broke down everything for me, letting me know how to go about the entire meeting. He placed emphasis that the most important thing is to not come across as an amateur and small minded, because if I did, it was a sure thing I would end up getting played. He advised that the best way to avoid that happening is to speak with confidence and try not to speak on anything I knew nothing about.

Before leaving D, we came to a mutual agreement that we become partners if everything went as planned. He would help me move the product, but that the prices had to be reasonable. D was already moving weight in Buffalo, Rochester and NYC so I figured he was just doing this as a favor to me, and I was determined not to let him down. My next move was to start recruiting my team, so I called up Clark and put him on to what was going down. When I told him the deal he immediately got enthused, letting me know he had my back 100%, and assured me that I could count on him regardless of anything. If everything went as planned on Friday I would definitely need some dependable dudes in my corner, and at this moment Clark and Kendu were ideal for the position.

CHAPTER 10

I was extremely happy by the time Friday rolled around, anxiously awaiting my meeting with Eric. Before leaving for the club I called up Eve to ensure everything was going as planned and she reassured me that Eric would, in fact, be there by the time I arrived. As I hung up the phone, I made sure to double check everything before leaving out the door. First impressions are generally a lasting one, therefore mine needed to be flawless. Upon arrival I checked my Michael Kors watch. I made it to the strip club in record time, a drive that generally took me 40 minutes, only took me 25. When I got to the entrance the bouncer let me in without asking any questions or searching me. I must admit, I thought that was kind of unusual for him not to search me, but I assumed he was expecting me anyways.

Entering the club, I walked over to the bar asking the bartender where I could find Eve. Before he could answer, I felt a tap on my shoulder. As I turned around, Eve was there standing behind me looking sexy as hell in a tan Gucci two piece that complimented her skin tone, giving her the look of a runway model.

Leaning towards me she placed a kiss on my cheek.

"Hey baby, what's going on, is your brother here yet?" I asked.

"No, but he should be here within the next couple minutes."

"Ok, so what do you want me to do until he gets here?"

"Just relax for a bit and order whatever you want. Drinks are on the house", she said, planting a succulent kiss on my lips before walking away heading to the back of the club.

As the Bartender made his way over to me I stated, "Let me get a rum and coke."

"One rum and coke coming up" He replied with a light smile.

One glass soon led to two and three before Eve made her way back to the bar, letting me know Eric had finally arrived and was ready to meet with me. She escorted me to an office located in the back of the club marked 'Employees Only'.

When we walked in, I saw two dudes sitting at a round table smoking what looked to be Cuban cigars. The younger of the two bore a striking resemblance to Eve, so I figured he had to be Eric. This was confirmed when we were introduced a few seconds later.

"Drew, this here is my big brother, Eric."

Eric got up out of his seat and embraced me, at the same time trying to intimidate me with his size. He was about 6 feet, stocky build with the body structure of an NFL linebacker. Surprisingly, when he spoke, he came off as a humble and soft-spoken individual. The other guy was introduced as Sammy, Eric's associate. After the introductions, both Eve and Sammy made their exit, leaving Eric and myself alone to get down to business.

Looking me directly in the eye Eric asked, "So Drew, what can I do for you?"

I replied, "What do you have that might be of use to me?" I could tell by the look on his face that my response caught him off guard and, to be honest, I surprised my damn self.

"Before we go any further Drew, I'd like to ask you a few questions, if you don't mind."

"No not at all. Shoot."

"Ok, I'm going to get straight to the point. What's the deal with you and my sister, and how do you really feel about her?"

"Well, at the moment we're just dating, but to be honest with you, I really do enjoy her company and I would love nothing more than for us to build on our relationship."

"I only hope you're being genuine for your own sake, and I want you to know that if it wasn't for my sister I wouldn't be meeting with you today. Mark my word; if you ever hurt my baby sister in any way whatsoever, I will see to it that you meet your Maker."

"Eric, you don't have to worry about that ever happening. The last thing I would ever think about doing is hurting her."

"Well, it's good to see that we're on the same page. Now let's talk business. What are you interested in: ecstasy, cocaine, heroin, or weed?"

The only drugs I came in contact with in the past were E pills and weed so I replied, "I was thinking about messing with weed and ecstasy right now. Those two seem to be the two most requested on the market. What are your prices on those products?" I asked.

"Well as far as pills, if you get them in bulk let's say a thousand or better, they go for $3 apiece; anything less you've got to pay $7 each. Now with weed I don't move no less than 20lbs at a time and it goes for $700 per pound, purple haze. Other than that, if you need me to transport it across the border, that would cost you $500 more for each shipment."

With prices like those I would be a fool not to jump on them. "So when can we get started?", I asked eager to get the process on the way.

"Whenever you're ready, just holla at me. Eve will give you my contacts."

"Okay, that sounds good to me. I'm going to finalize everything with my people and get back to you in a few days."

"Yo Drew, make sure you know what you are getting yourself into. Eve mentioned that you're in school. Why would you want to jeopardize your future for this? You seem like a smart enough individual Papi. You don't need to get involved in this lifestyle," he said in his Dominican accent.

Right away I thought to myself, "This dude is right on the money with what he just said." I knew I was in way over my head right now, but I thought, "What the hell. I've already come this far, there ain't no way I was gonna turn back now."

"To be honest with you Eric, times are hard for me right now and this seems like the only way I can make some real money."

"I understand where you're coming from. Just try to be careful, and make sure you know what you're doing. The worst thing you can do is come into this game with a blindfold on."

I replied, "Good looking out, man. I really do appreciate you coming at me the way you just did. Most dudes wouldn't really care about anyone else as long as they got their money. But I promise I will take what you just said in consideration."

"Ok Drew, I guess I'll be hearing from you within the next couple of days."

"You most definitely will," I replied as I got up and shook his hands before leaving the office.

When I went back out front, I headed straight for the bar, anxiously awaiting Eve while engulfed in deep thought. There was absolutely no stopping me now. The only thing I had to do was come up with enough money to cover the first shipment.

So far, I had a little over $17000 saved up for my truck. I could probably ask my parents, but they would end up asking too many questions, trying to figure out what I needed it for. Or I could ask Eve to spot me the money; it was obvious she was holding. She had a brother who was a drug lord and an uncle who ran a strip joint that, without a doubt, brought in mad money. It should be nothing for her to loan me a couple thousand dollars. The only thing that stopped me from going to her was my pride and ego. I didn't want her looking at me as a sucker or a scrub.

Within seconds Eve appeared from the dressing room smiling ear to ear and asked, "So how was it?"

"It actually went better than I expected. Thanks to you, of course", I replied returning the smile.

"I am happy for you baby. So, am I going to see you when I get off of work?"

"I honestly doubt it, hun. I've got to head back to Long Island to get up with my homies to discuss business."

"Oh ok, I was really trying to spend the night with you, but if you got things to take care of I understand."

"Alright sweetie, how about you come to Long Island tonight after work?"

"Drew, are you sure you won't have no other females over there?" she asked smiling.

"Yeah, I'm positive. Unless you trying to experiment a little." I exclaimed with a smirk.

"No, I don't think so, you freak, I'll see you later." She replied leaning over to plant a kiss on my cheek.

CHAPTER 11

When I made it back to Long Island, I called up Simone
before doing anything else. She had called me numerous
times today, leaving messages for me to holla at her and I
hadn't, so I knew for a fact that I was going to be cursed
out. I figured I might as well get it over with now, instead
of waiting until later. When I called, her voicemail came on
after the 5th ring. I was about to leave her a message, but
changed my mind and opted to check her messages instead.
After about a couple of months in our relationship, we both
came to an agreement that we would exchange each other's
pass codes just to ensure that we don't keep any secrets
from one another. I must admit when she first brought up
the idea, I thought it was ludicrous, but after a while I gave
in just to make her happy. After putting in her pass code the
recording came on notifying me that there was only one
new message received at 1am from a Carl. Hearing this
only peaked my interest more so I pressed for the message
to be played. Immediately after an unfamiliar voice came
over the phone saying "Hey Simone, this is Carl. I'm just
calling to let you know that I had fun last night and I've
been thinking about you like crazy ever since."

Hearing this message caused me to become furious. This
bitch couldn't be serious! I just know she wasn't stupid
enough to go out there and cheat on me. Before I went any
further and did something I might end up regretting, I
calmed down a little and decided to try to get in contact
with her first to get some answers.

After four failed attempts to reach her on her cell phone, I tried her house phone. To my surprise, her mother picked up on the second ring "Hello, who is this?"

"It's me Drew, Mrs. Brown. I'm really sorry for calling your home this late, but it's very important that I speak to Simone."

"Is everything alright Drew?"

"Yes and no. I just need to find out something from Simone. Do you know if she is up?"

"I honestly don't know, but hold on a sec while I check."

A minute or so later Simone's voice came over the phone sounding concerned.

"Hi baby is everything okay?"

"Who the hell is Carl, Simone, and why the heck he calling you at 1 o'clock in the morning?"

The silence that followed gave me my answer, so I continued where I left off, barking at her through the phone, "How could you play me like this Simone? I gave you my all and this is how you repay me? It's my fault anyways for putting my trust in your trifling ass in the first place."

"What are you talking about Drew?"

"Don't act stupid with me. You know what I'm talking about. Who the hell is Carl and what were you doing chilling with him? You know what Simone, fuck you, you ain't nothing but a slut anyways, goodbye and don't try calling me back."

I hung up the phone immediately after not even giving her the opportunity to respond. For the next couple of minutes my phone kept on ringing as Simone tried relentlessly in hopes I would pick up. When she finally gave up I had a total of 17 new messages from her. Deep down I knew that I was being a hypocrite because I was doing the exact thing she was, the only difference was that I didn't get caught, she did. In my heart I wanted to forgive her but my ego and pride wouldn't allow me to. There was just no way we could be together after what had just happened. Our relationship was starting to go sour anyways so I figured something like this would happen eventually. By the time I made it home it was already two in the morning. I figured D would be sleeping by now so I called and left him a message, letting him know that everything went as planned, and to buzz me back in the am. Immediately after I called Clark. He answered on the second ring. "Yo Drew, what's good?"

"Ain't shit. I got some good news?"

"So why you sounding like that?"

"Well I just broke up with Simone, but that's old news. Let's get down to what's important. I met with dude and everything went smooth."

"That's what's up bro."

"Well he's willing to supply us with whatever we need and the prices are irresistible. I told him I'd get back to him as soon as I came up with the money, so we got to meet up tomorrow and talk some more."

"No doubt, we'll definitely do that."

My cell phone began beeping letting me know I had an incoming call, so I told Clark to hold on while I checked to see who it was.

When I clicked over, it was Eve letting me know she was on her way.

After Eve hung up I switched over to resume my convo with Clark and heard him in the background speaking to Kendu.

"Yo Clark, I'm back" I yelled over the phone, in an effort to get his attention.

"Oh, my bad, son. This fool Kendu was bugging me, trying to figure out what was going on," he replied.

"Aight, we've got to hook up first thing tomorrow to bring everyone up to date and get shit sorted out."

"Aight Drew, I'll spread the word to everyone else."

Things were falling into place exactly how I needed them to. I just needed my team to execute with no fuck ups.

By the time Eve got to my place, I had just made it out the shower and was wrapped in a towel from the waist down, exposing my ripped upper body. At first glance she exclaimed, "Damn baby, you ain't gotta be flaunting all that in my face! You couldn't have waited for me to hop in the shower, huh?"

I smiled and replied, "I'm sorry baby, I promise I'll make it up to you."

She smirked playfully and said, "Yeah, whatever Drew. I'm about to go take a shower. If you want to, you could come and join me."

"That's okay baby, I'll be laying in bed, waiting for you", I replied.

"Ok then, it's your loss, not mines", she said and strolled into the bathroom.

Right away, the thought of one of my housemates getting up to use the bathroom while she was in there taking a shower crossed my mind, forcing me to go join her. The last thing I wanted was one of my perverted ass housemates looking at my girl while she took a shower. When I walked into the bathroom, I made sure to turn the lock on the door to ensure we weren't interrupted by anyone. Making my way over to the tub, I parted the shower curtain just to get a better view of what was behind it, causing Eve to turn around surprised.

When she saw that it was me she began smiling and said "It's good to see that you changed your mind."

I was turned on by her nakedness immediately as she stood there with water running down the crevices of her body.

The towel that was once draped around me was now on the floor. Upon entering the tub my expectation was that she would take me in her arms, but she surprised me as she turned off the water and knelt in front me. Starting at the tops of my feet, she gradually kissed, caressed, nibbled and licked her way up to my upper body. As she made her way up the crease between my thighs, she stopped and kissed my penis momentarily, causing me to become fully erect. Making her way up to my chest, her mouth lingered on each nipple, pulling it tenderly at the tip. With each pull my toes curled from the sensation. She finally made her way up to my lips and kissed me, long, deep and hard. Her eyes followed me expectantly as I knelt slowly in front her worshiping every aspect of her nakedness. Extending my tongue to meet her vagina, I kissed and licked her clit, humming on the tip to give off a vibrating sensation, causing her knees to buckle. This caused her excitement to trickle down my nose. She immediately began squirming with pleasure as she placed her hands on my head to push my mouth closer to her honeycomb.

Looking up at her I saw the expression of torturous pleasure. That was my cue to intensify my actions. Seeing the pleasure on her face had my dick throbbing, wanting to be inside her, but now wasn't the time. I wanted her to cum uncontrollably on the tip of my tongue, and I had no intentions of stopping until I accomplished my task. Her clit was now being consumed by my lips as I continued sucking and licking while using two fingers to keep the rest of her vagina occupied.

Within seconds her legs started shivering as she erupted in multiple orgasms, trying relentlessly to push my head away but to no avail. I wanted her to fully enjoy what I was doing. After she came three more times I was satisfied; job well done. Turning away from me she leaned over facing the wall, spreading her legs wide and inviting me to enter her place of comfort.

"Drew, I want you to fuck me, I want you to beat this pussy up, Papi." she demanded.

I wasted no time doing as I was told, positioning myself directly behind her, easing all of my love muscle inside her wetness, causing Eve to gasp for air. I began grinding inside her making deep thrusts in an effort to find her g-spot, causing her to become extremely vocal, moaning in ecstasy.

Placing my hand on her ass I began spanking her with one hand as I used the other to stimulate her more by rubbing on her clit.

"Whose pussy is this?" I asked while I spanked her ass, causing it to jiggle even more with ever slap.

"It's yours daddy."

I wasn't satisfied with her answer so I asked her again, "Whose is it?"

This time she answered, "It's all yours Drew, this pussy belongs to you."

Seconds became minutes and time elapsed as we were consumed in ecstasy. Making our way out the shower, I picked her up and placed her on top of the bathroom sink, continuing where we had left off. Tears began streaming down her cheeks as she looked at me and said "sweetie, I am really falling in love with you, but I'm scared I might end up getting hurt."

"Baby, you don't ever have to worry about that", I replied meaning every last word. Within seconds, her entire body began shaking as she climaxed for the fifth time. The sensation was so breathtaking that I found myself on the verge of climaxing. Sensing that I was about to cum, Eve whispered, "Baby, I want you to come inside me."

She didn't have to tell me twice, and the sensation that rippled through my body wouldn't allow anything else. My hips tightened and my toes curled as I erupted inside her, "I'mmmm Cummmmmminn"

Lovemaking never felt this good before. "Was this truly love I was feeling?" I questioned myself.

Leaning forward I planted a long, wet kiss on her lips saying, "Baby, I love you with all my heart."

That night we made love over and over again until we became exhausted and passed out. For some reason, I was kind of apprehensive at first to unveil my true feelings to her, but after that night, it was a thing of the past. It was now official, and I wanted the whole world to know that I was in love with Eve.

The following morning, I woke up to the sound of my cell phone going off. The phone number showed up as being unavailable so I figured it was Simone calling to bother me. I was contemplating on letting my voicemail answer, but opted to take the call.

"Hello, who is this?" I asked sounding irritated.

"Bro it's me D, what's good?"

"Besides you interrupting my beauty nap, nothing much."

He began laughing then said, "Drew you are a clown for real."

"Well I'm assuming you called to find out what the deal was so let's cut to the chase" I said with a light chuckle. "I met with dude last night and everything went great. I told him that I was only interested in trees and E pills, and the prices are official."

"That sounds good. So how would we get the goods from him?"

"Well this is where everything gets better; he is willing to transport whatever we need for only a small cost".

"Oh ok, so how much money will we need to get started?"

"Well I was thinking somewhere in the ballpark of $50, 000."

"That's a lot of money Drew."

"Yeah, I know, but the prices are cheap as hell, and at the same time I'm not trying to step to dude half-assed with no bullshit that might end up flopping us before we even get our feet in the door."

"I see where you're coming from. Just make sure you're making the right decision."

"I got you D; just trust me on this one."

"Ok, I'm going to take your word for it. Well how about I send you 25 g's and we make this a 50/50 business venture?"

I was kind a skeptical about his offer, but at the time I didn't have much of a choice, so I agreed. "Aight bro, I could work with that."

"So, what do you plan on getting as a start up?"

"I was thinking about 50lbs a weed, at $700 apiece and 5000 pills at $3 a pop."

"Sounds good to me. Well, I'm gonna send my little man over there with my half. I just hope everything goes as planned, and make sure you holla at me as soon as you get it so we can get this thing in motion."

"Aight my dude, peace."

As I made it off the phone I noticed a note on top of my dresser from Eve, letting me know she had to head home to handle some business, also professing her love for me. Reading her note put a smile on my face. Nothing could possibly go wrong. I had the girl of the dreams and I was getting ready to make some major paper.

Reaching for my cell phone I called Clark to set up a meeting. We agreed to meet up at his apartment around 2 o'clock, and I told him to ensure Abdul and Kendu were there also. I had a couple hours to burn before our meeting so I got out of bed, made myself something to eat and showered before leaving the apartment.

By the time I arrived at Clark's crib, everyone was there clowning around, waiting for my arrival. After greeting each other, we got down to business right away. I broke everything down to them in detail and put them all on to the fact that what we were about to get ourselves into could be risky and at the same time deadly. So, going around in a circle I asked everyone if they were willing to go the distance; and one after the other they answered; YES.

That day we formed a bond and agreed that we would never turn our backs on each other; it was death before dishonor always.

"Yo Drew, we got to find a name for ourselves," Kendu stated.

Abdul replied "How about Bashment Crew?"

We all yelled, "Oh hell nah!" in unison.

"So Drew, what do you have in mind?" Clark asked.

"I don't know. How about High Rollaz?"

"Yeah, I kinda like the sound of that, it could definitely work" Kendu replied.

"Aight its official, from now on we're going to go by High Rollaz."

One after the other we got up, slapping each other high fives, giving our crew's name our seal of approval.

The conversation soon shifted to the most important thing at the moment, money. After taking note of what everyone in the room could come up with and calculating it, we came up with a total of $21,500, so we still needed to come up with $3500 more. Clark then stated "Yo, I know how we could get the rest of the money, but we got to wait until later on tonight."

"What are you talking about?" I asked.

"Well I now this dude that sells weed out of his apartment over on the west side, and I know for a fact he is holding. We could easily make out with 10g's not to mention drugs."

"So what's the deal?" I asked becoming more interested.

"Well, all we got to do is stake out his apartment, and whenever he makes it to his front door we just run up on him and force him inside. I know where his stash is and all that."

"Bro, that shit sounds too good to be true." Abdul stated.

I replied "Yo whatever son, right about now we don't have any other options."

"So what time are you all trying to do this?"

Clark answered and said "Anytime between 12 and 1 tonight. I'm going to give him a call in a little while to make sure he is still going out to the bars tonight, and then we'll take it from there."

We all agreed that we would hook up and meet back up at Clark's later on to finalize everything before we went our separate ways.

CHAPTER 12

By the time one am rolled around, we were already parked a couple houses away from dude's crib, patiently waiting for his return from the bar. The bar was only three blocks away from his apartment so we could easily spot him walking back. We were all posted up in a crackhead's car we had gotten earlier, dressed in all black with the hoods from our sweatshirts pulled over our heads, concealing our identities with ski-masks. We also came strapped, just in case he had company and they needed to be subdued for any reason. A couple minutes later Clark tapped me on my shoulder saying, "Yo Drew, I think that might be him walking this way."

"Are you sure about that bro?"

"Yea that's him, I'm positive."

Luckily for us, he was by himself, apparently drunk, stumbling and singing. The dude was relatively short, no taller than 5'5", slender and he looked completely harmless. As soon as he made it to his front door I got out of the car with Clark in tow, making sure we weren't seen by anyone. Running up on him, I pulled my 9mm, placing it on his neck.

"Yo, open the motherfucking door and try not to make a scene, or else I'll blow your brains out."

He chose not to put up any resistance, which was the right thing to do. As he opened the door, I pushed him to the floor and directed Clark to close the door and secure the premises to make sure there wouldn't be any surprises. Within seconds the front door opened up as Abdul and Kendu walked in with guns in hand. I turned to the fellas, advising them to check the rest of the house while I dealt with our prisoner.

All of a sudden, he began crying and begging for his life, "Please don't hurt me man, anything you want you can have, just please don't hurt me."

Hearing his whining only made me aggravated, so I ordered him to shut the hell up.

"You know what we're here for so just give it up and there won't be any problems"

I could tell that he was petrified as I said those words to him with my gun pointed directly to his face. I then ordered him to stand up so I could search him.

He was a bit apprehensive as he got up off the floor, so I figured something must be up. When I checked his waist to see if he was strapped, I was surprised to find a loaded 357 magnum inside his pants. I immediately ordered him to take me to the money after relieving him of the pistol. He was now disarmed of the only hope he had for retaliation, so he led me directly to his stash and gave me what we came to get. After our goal was accomplished, I directed Abdul and Kendu to tie him up and duct-tape him so he wouldn't cause any problems. This was as easy as 1-2-3 and a job well done.

On my way of the door, I heard bang bang. Immediately, I spun around with my gun drawn, shocked and trying to figure out what the hell just happened. When I looked around, I saw Abdul standing with his gun in hand, aimed directly at the dudes' head, while he lay motionless on the floor.

"What the fuck just happened?" I asked, looking dumbfounded inhaling the smell of gunpowder that encompassed the room.

"Yo Drew, that fool tried to make a move on me so I popped him", he replied.

"Aight bro, what's done is done. Let's get the hell outta here while we still can.", I exclaimed shaking my head in disbelief.

"Aight, I'm just going to wipe down the crib real quick to make sure there ain't nothing left to link us to this shit."

A night that began with plans of just making some extra money to fund our little business venture, just turned into a robbery and homicide.

To my knowledge neither of us had ever killed anyone before, so this was definitely going to be life altering from this night forward, and it was evident that there was nothing good to come in the future.

CHAPTER 13

Upon arriving at the crib, we calculated everything we took from the work we just put in. We made out with a total of $13,000 and 3lbs of weed and a 357 magnum. After what happened tonight, I knew that there would be no turning back for any of us. We were in too deep. It was a proven fact that once you kill, you're likely to do it again. We ended up coming to an agreement that what happened tonight would stay between us only, no matter what. The High Rollaz were now on the come up and there would be no stopping us at this point. I decided to wait until the next morning to give Eric a call to finalize our business transaction. Tonight, me and my team were going to have some fun and celebrate a little. My roommate Maine was DJing at a college party at the Sphere nightclub downtown, so we decided to check it out. Shit, after all that took place tonight we for sure needed to unwind a bit.Upon arrival at the club, all eyes were on us as we made our entrance. It was an hour or so before closing so we wasted no time getting our club on. There were beautiful women in abundance getting their groove on, and we were determined to get with a couple before the night was out. The club was relatively huge and a popular night spot. There were two floors, with the main dance-floor located on the first floor and the DJ booth and the bar was on the second floor with the V.I.P. section.

Moments later, we made it up to the second floor where the ballers and groupies were at. The first thing that caught my attention was a group of females surrounding three dudes sitting to the left of the DJ booth with bottles of Moët everywhere. I was determined to top whatever they had, so I made my way over to the bar with the fellas in tow. We all sat by the bar for the next couple minutes ordering bottles of Hpnotiq and Hennessey, getting drunk and acting a fool, slowly gaining the attention of everyone around us. That night, we were being admired by the ladies and hated on by all the fellas. I ordered a bottle of Moët and took it over to Maine in the DJ booth located on stage.

"Yo what's good, my dude? I see you doing you. You got the entire club on smash" I yelled over the music to ensure he heard me.

"Yo good looking out, son. I'm just doing my job, ya heard," Maine replied with a smile.

"Yeah aight. Well, I'm a let you do your thing, but do me a favor and shout out the High Rollaz for me."

"Who's that?" he asked.

"That's my crew. I'll fill you in later."

"Aight son, I got you, and thanks for the bottle"

"No doubt bro, just keep up the good work," I replied giving Maine a dap.

Maine was, without a doubt, one of the best DJ's in town, and he always knew how to keep the party jumping all night, which also boosted his popularity with the females.

Minutes later his voice came over the speakers saying, "Right about now, I want everyone on the dance floor fi start Syvah, but before that I want to shout out my dudes, Da High Rollaz crew in the building. Champagne popping it; you know how we do".

Ding Dong's smash hit "Syvah, oh my days" came on next, causing everyone in the club to start dancing.

Upon hearing our crew name over the speakers, we became hyped and at the same time sparking up our blunts. There was no stopping us now; we were about to be on top of our game. The High Rollaz were in the building in full force and here to stay. By the time the lights came on signaling closing, both Kendu and Clark had already gotten rides back to their apartments, so it was just Abdul and myself left out of the crew.

While making our way out of the club, I heard a familiar voice calling my name, so I turned to around to see who it was.

When I did I saw Shameka, Michelle's house mate walking over to me looking sexy as hell.

"Hey Drew, how are you?"

"I'm good, what's going on with you?"

"Nothing much, I might need a favor from you, if you don't mind me asking."

I automatically thought that this gold-digging bitch was trying to get me for some money, but opted to say, "What's up go ahead, shoot."

"Well, Michelle and Lona left me to go home earlier and now I am stuck without a way home. This guy I know offered me a ride, but I would rather if you took me home, if that's ok with you"

She was looking too good for me to turn her down, and who knew what this might lead to, so I turned to her and said "Aight then, are you ready to go now?"

She replied "Yeah, whenever you are."

"Oh, before I forget, I'm gonna have to drop my boy home before you because his place is closer."

"Don't worry about it, I'm in no rush." She stated biting on her bottom lip.

When we made it to the car, I checked my cell phone to see if I had my any missed calls. The only message I had was from my ex letting me know that she still loved me. After the fight we had, we spoke about what happened like two responsible adults and reconciled our differences. It was undeniable that I still had strong feelings for her, but we needed a break from each other. My grandmother always told me that sometimes you've got to let go of the person you love and if it is was meant to be that person will come right back eventually. I viewed all this as a test to see how strong our love for each other really was.

CHAPTER 14

After dropping off Abdul, we cruised down Caldena Rd on the way to Shameka's place.

Reaching into the glove compartment I grabbed a CD that would be ideal for the mood. The music began taking over our emotions immediately. Silk's hit song "There's a meeting in my bedroom.", echoed softly out the speakers.

Peering out the corner of my eye, I caught Shameka staring at me. When she realized I had caught her she turned to me and said, "Drew, what do you have planned for the rest of the night?"

"I don't know. I might just head back to the crib and chill. What about you?" I asked.

"I'm not sure, I'm not even tired or anything."

Right away I thought to myself, "If I was ever going to make a move, now would be the perfect time to do so". So, I turned to her and asked if she wanted to come chill with me. Without hesitation she replied, "I don't see why not, but you've got to promise to have me home before daybreak."

"Aight no problem," I replied.

That's all I needed to hear coming from her mouth. Without hesitation I made a sudden U-turn heading for my love palace.

When we got to the crib, I checked to make sure my housemates weren't home, because I wasn't trying to be interrupted.

Just like clockwork, upon entering my bedroom she pushed me up against the door and stuck her hand down my pants, pulling out my love muscle and stroking it gently.

"Drew, I've wanted to do this for a long time," she said whispering in my ear.

"Me too, baby."

I was so caught up in the heat of the moment that my words weren't even coming out properly. In seconds, her clothes had fallen to the floor, revealing her perky nipples. I began sucking and licking on them eagerly, while my hands ventured into forbidden places. After a minute or so of foreplay, I couldn't fight the urge any longer. I needed to be inside her, and I could tell that she yearned for the same. She then grabbed my dick, squeezing it firmly as she guided it to the entrance of her vagina. Her warmth enveloped me like a glove as I drove deep into her, while she gasped with anticipation of my next move. I began pumping in and out of her as her hand gripped my ass while we stroked each other, moving in tandem. We went at it for hours, orgasm after orgasm, until we both had enough. We laid there for a few minutes trying to recoup. Thoughts began flowing through my mind. What was I doing messing around with this chick when I was in love with Eve? I felt as if I was doing too much and needed to calm down and take my relationship more serious before I ended up losing the love of my life.

Looking over at Shameka I asked, "Hey, you ready to go?"

With a smile on her face she uttered, "Yea, let me get dressed.

The entire ride on my way to drop her off was rather silent. Deep down we both enjoyed the sex, but knew that would be the first and last time we would ever hook up.

After dropping her off, I headed straight home to get some rest for my big day tomorrow.

On the way home I received a call from Eve, which I found somewhat puzzling.

"Hey Drew, where are you? I have something important to show you?"

Her statement peaked my curiosity. Before uttering a word, I made an immediate u turn.

"I'm on my way baby, hold tight"

K, my love. See you soon".

Upon arrival, it appeared Eve was crying previously which had me very concerned. Is everything ok?

She led me to the bathroom sink, neglecting to answer my previous question. What I saw on top the counter had me speechless. Staring aimlessly at the plus sign I turned to her and asked; "Are we pregnant?"

Tears of joy and apprehension began streaming down her cheeks, while she peered into my eyes looking for confirmation of my happiness.

Things were definitely falling into place and having a child on the way will be the ultimate game changer in our lives.

Gently pulling her closer to me I held her hands and placed a reassuring kiss on her forehead. "I want you to be my wife Eve", I stated on impulse.

"Are you sure Drew, you want us to get married?"

"Yes darling, I want you to be mine forever", I said meaning every word.

That night we sat and spoke about future plans along with baby name until fell asleep with her in my arms.

CHAPTER 15

The following morning, I woke up filled with joy and anxious to get my operation on the way. I was a 21-year-old college student on the verge of being a father, a husband, a drug dealer, and, I was determined to do what I had to do not to be a failure. After getting dressed, I sat and ate breakfast with my fiancé, putting her on to my plans for the day.

As I headed to the front door on my way out, Eve held my hand. She looked me in the eyes and whispered concerningly, "Good luck, and be careful."

"Thanks baby, and I most definitely will", I stated placing a soft kiss on her lips before making my exit.

The shipment was scheduled to arrive later on today, so I had to make sure everything was in order. The first thing I did was call D to figure out how we would transport the product and where we would store it. We agreed to mask the drugs at one of his stash spots over on Guy-R-Brower and also in Flatbush, and that we would get a U-Haul truck to transport it. I got off the phone with him to meet my crew, making sure that everything was in order and that the street soldiers were ready to go. When I got to Clark's crib, Abdul and Kendu were already there with five other dudes they introduced me to as Black, Papa Shot, Shizzle, Kevon and Papa Smurf. All five of these dudes were straight grimmey, hood cats who were willing to bust their guns at any given time. Clark reassured me that they were some of his most loyal soldiers and that they could be trusted, so I took his word for it. The craziest thing about these dudes was that they were all related in some way. Kevon, Shizzle, Papa Shot, and Papa Smurf were all brothers and Black was a distant cousin of theirs. Both Papa Shot and Shizzle were known as the gun slingers, while Black, Smurf and Kevon were the thinkers and natural-born hustlers. They were all going to play a major role in this organization. Both Papa Shot and Shizzle would be stationed as enforcers for the dudes I'll have hustling on the corners, while Kevon, Black and Smurf would be pumping at the local colleges, bars and night clubs.

So, all in all, we had everything pretty much organized and ready to take off.

By 11pm, we were at the warehouse on Broadway parked in the front with my little man Black in a U-Haul truck a few yards away waiting for the pick-up. We made sure to pick this spot to ensure we weren't easily noticed by any outsiders. This building was stationed on a one-way street, so traffic wasn't really an issue to us. Within seconds, my cell phone rang. It was Eric calling to let me know they had arrived. As I got off the phone, I saw a black Suburban pull into the parking lot with a tractor trailer in tow. I then got out of my car to go meet Eric as I saw him getting out his truck. When I made it over to him, we embraced and got down to business right after.

"Let's take care of this so we can hurry up and get out of here, E," I said with a smile on my face.

"Sounds good to me, Drew. Well, the product is inside the trailer packaged as boxes of vegetables. It's all there: 60lbs of weed and 7000 E pills. If you want, you could check to make sure of that."

Right away I knew he basically said that to see what my reaction would be so I replied, "Naw that's aight, Eric, I trust you." I then handed him a duffle bag filled with $51,000 as he smiled and said, "Drew, I like how you do business."

Meanwhile, the boys had already checked the goods and unloaded them onto the U-Haul. Pleased with how everything went we shook hands momentarily and made our exits. Step 1 of the hustle was complete, it was now time to execute. When we made it back to the stash spot we began bagging up the product right away. We broke down the weed to pounds, ounces, quarter pounds, eight's, 10's and 20's. As far as the pills went, we set aside double stacks, triple stacks, singles and stacks of ten. That night we stayed up and made sure we had everything organized. There was absolutely no room for error. We would be selling pounds for $3,500, ounces for $300, quarter pounds for $1000 and everything else we bagged up for 10's, 20's and eights. As for the pills, we were selling them at $10 each and $7 a piece wholesale. It was guaranteed we would make a killing because everyone else was selling their pills for $15-$25. We already had a couple blocks to work with over on Linden and Merrick, and at the same time we had the college campuses on smash, meanwhile D had his customers from Corporate America, so all in a all every area was well covered.

"Aye yow fellas, I'm about to take it down, so I'll holla at y'all tomorrow," I stated as I got up, making my way towards the front door.

Before I made my exit, I turned to them and yelled enthused, "Let's get money, my dudes. High Rollaz for life!"

CHAPTER 16

On my way home, I checked my messages to see if anyone had tried to get in contact with me since I had my phone off for the majority of the day. In all, I had three new messages. The first new message was from my pops telling me to give them a call to let them know whether or not I was going to make it home in time for our annual summer vacation to Virginia. I had so many things on my agenda to take care of at this present moment, it was almost impossible for me to make it to Virginia this summer; and at the same time, I needed to have a serious talk with my parents to notify them on the fact that they were going to be grandparents, and that I was getting married. The second message I received came from Michelle, letting me know it was very important that I see her as soon as possible. Right away, I thought to myself, "No, this bitch Shameka didn't go running her mouth to Michelle about what happened, because, if she had, I would have to break her damn neck."

The third and final message was from my baby's mother and wife to be inquiring if everything went as planned and letting me know she missed me and loved me. As soon as I finished checking my voicemails, I dialed up Eve. She answered on the second ring, "Hey baby, how was your day? You know you had me worrying about you." Hearing her words of concern made me smile as I replied, "Isn't that sweet. Baby, everything went as planned, it couldn't have been better. I'm sorry I didn't get to call you earlier. I kind of figured Eric would've called and let you know how everything went."

"He actually did, but I still needed to hear it coming from you baby. You know the last thing I would want is for something to happen to my husband."

I smiled then replied, "I'll make sure nothing happens to either one of us, baby, and that's a promise. By the way, what are you wearing? I definitely wouldn't mind getting another taste of what I got the other night."

She chuckled lightly and said, "Is that so? Well, right now I got your Polo T-shirt on and a pair of your sweats.

"Oh, I can only imagine how crazy your hail look," I said, laughing at my own joke.

"Why don't you come and take what is rightfully yours?" she said playfully.

"I wish I could baby, but I still got some unfinished business to take care of for the night." I was lying my ass off because in the back of my mind I was planning to stop by Michelle's crib to see her before I went home.

"Baby, I promise you we will get up tomorrow and spend some quality time together."

She replied and said, "Ok babe. Anyways, we need to seriously start making plans to get an apartment together."

Her statement left me completely speechless. The idea of us having to share a home together never really crossed my mind before. My player days were definitely on the verge of coming to an end and there was absolutely nothing I could do about it.

I was jarred from my thoughts by Eve's voice coming over the phone, trying to get my attention, "Drew, are you there baby?"

"Yeah, hun, I'm here. This fool made a sudden stop in front of me, causing me to slam on my brakes and I dropped the phone." I lied, trying not to seem too taken a back from her statement.

"Oh ok, are you alright?"

"Yes baby, I'm good. "

"Alright then, go take care of what you have to and be safe, and make sure you get some sleep. Talk to you tomorrow and don't forget about what I said."

"Aight sweetie, I love you."

"I love you more Drew. Bye."

I needed someone to talk to, someone I could confide in and express myself freely without being criticized and the only person I could lean on in that way is Michelle. So, when I got off the phone with Eve, I called up Michelle letting her know I was headed her way and to look out for me.

CHAPTER 17

Upon arrival, I automatically sensed something was wrong just by the way Michelle greeted me with a nod of her head instead of the usual hug we would share. I was just hoping it wasn't what I thought it was. As soon as we got to her bedroom, I turned to her and asked, "Mich, what's the matter? What's so important that you needed to speak to me urgently?"

"Drew, I don't know how to break this to you gently, so I'm just gonna come straight out and say it. Baby, I'm 2 months pregnant. I've been meaning to tell you, but every time I see you, you're there with someone or just too busy to stop and talk."

The first words that escaped my mouth were, "Are you sure about this Michelle? How do you know?"

"Yes Drew, I am 100% positive. I went to the doctor a couple days ago and they confirmed."

"So, what do you plan on doing?" I asked.

"I don't know Drew, I'm just scared. I do want to have this baby, but at the same time, I'm worried about what my parents will have to say."

"I'm truly sorry hun for putting you in such a fucked-up predicament, but whatever you choose to do, I'll be there for you all the way."

Tears started rolling down her cheeks as she said, "I love you baby, and if I do decide to keep this child, I would love nothing more than for you to play a major part in this child's life."

"I promise I'll be there every step of the way for you and our child, but there is something I need to let you know before we go any further."

"What is it, Drew?"

"Well, do you remember me telling you I was seeing a chick from New Rochelle?"

"Yeah, what does she have to do with anything?"

"Well, I found out recently that she's also pregnant, and we're engaged to be married."

My statement really hit her hard and she began crying uncontrollably. I immediately walked over to her sitting on the bed, reassuring her that no matter what happened, I'd always be there for her and the baby. That night we made love for the last time. We both knew that the love we had for each other would never die and our bond would only be stronger now with a baby on the way, but at the same time I was engaged to be married to Eve and neither one of us wanted to upset those plans.

After she fell asleep in my arms, I just lay there, staring into space with numerous thoughts running through my mind. As of today, my life was about to make a drastic transition from Drew the college boy, to Drew the drug dealer, father of two, and husband to be. Without a doubt, I had to step my shit up and I had to do so quick.

CHAPTER 18

After the first week of operation, we ran through our entire
product, totaling our profits at over $300,000. I wasted no
time contacting Eric to re-up, this time copping 100lbs of
haze and 10,000 E pills. D was now getting rid of a total of
4,000 E pills and up to 30lbs of haze per week, while my
team ran through the rest with ease.

Within no time, we had all of Jamaica Queens on smash,
not mention Smurf, Kevon and Black had the college
campuses on lock and flooded with our product. Everyone
was eating, and the name High Rollaz was definitely out
there. Whenever anyone heard about the High Rollaz, they
thought of some real, official money-getters.With our
popularity and success on the rise, we were accumulating
haters on an everyday basis. So, we now had to worry
about the cops, stick up kids and the snitches. We just had
to deal with whatever obstacles as they came up. The
spring semester had now come to an end, and I surprisingly
pulled through with a 3.2 GPA. I had the entire summer to
get my life together, to build my organization and to work
on my family.

Still, I had not told my parents the fact that they were about
to be grandparents and that I was getting married, but I
knew I could not hide it from them much longer. They
needed to know, and real soon. I had set aside today to
celebrate my accomplishments with Eve and also to go
shopping for a home, so I made sure to let my crew know
not to holla at me unless it was of great importance; today

was solely for me and the wife. After taking my shower, I got ready and left my apartment on my way to go get Eve in New Rochelle. We had come to an agreement that she would not be stripping anymore since she was pregnant and she stayed true to her word. Ever since then, she would spend a lot more time home or out shopping and doing things like going to the salon to get her hair and nails done.

When I pulled up to her driveway, I saw a brand new, all white 2014 Yukon Denali truck parked right next to her Mercedes Benz convertible. I automatically thought it belonged to her brother or uncle so I shrugged it off as nothing. Seconds later, she came running through the front door looking sexy as hell in a pink tank top, blue Seven jeans, and a pair of pink Gucci heels, which brought out her beauty and sex appeal even more. She definitely knew how to carry herself and I loved that about her. She embraced me, placing her succulent lips on mine, giving me a warm and gentle kiss.

"Hey baby, it's good to see you."

"It's good to see you too. You look beautiful. Who is here with you?"

She replied, "No one, why do you ask that?"

"Then whose truck is that?" I asked pointing towards the Yukon.

"It's yours, baby," she replied with a smile on her face. "I wanted to do something special for you and I knew how much you wanted a truck, so I decided to surprise you with this."

I was so overcome with happiness that I picked her up and spun her around saying, "Thank you very much babe, but you know you didn't have to do all this for me."

"Drew, there is nothing is this world I wouldn't do for you, baby. You deserve nothing but the best."

Reaching into her back pocket, she pulled out the keys and handed them to me. "Go check it out. The title, license, insurance and registration are all in the glove compartment."

When I walked over to the truck and opened it, I felt like a kid in a candy store. The truck was sitting on 22" rims, while the inside was plush with black and white leather interior, TVs in the headrest, a banging sound system, Xbox game console, navigational system and a stash box she had installed for my business purposes. I could do nothing but smile as I turned to her, planted a kiss on her forehead and said, "Thank you very much, sweetheart."

"You're welcome, daddy. "Just give me a second to go lock up so we can be on our way."

"OK, beautiful, I'll be here waiting."

On the ride back to Long Island all I could think of was riding around in my new car and seeing the look on my boys' faces, they were going to shit themselves.

Our first stop was at a townhouse in Amityville over on Longmeadow Road. D had put me onto this spot, telling me it was a steal and guaranteeing that I would love it so I wanted to see for myself if he was right.

When we pulled up to the house my first impression was that it was a good neighborhood, and if the inside of the house was as appealing as the outside, we would definitely take it on the spot. The house was situated on the corner of Longmeadow Road and University Avenue, so the yard was really huge, with flower beds surrounding it. There was also a children's play area and a pool located in the backyard with a two-car garage at the side of the house.

The inside of the house was just as expected. There was a total of three bedrooms, two bathrooms, a kitchen, living room and a dining room. The master bathroom had a Jacuzzi and bathtub. The house was absolutely breathtaking.

As soon as we finished the tour of the house Eve turned to me and said, "Baby, this is it! This is where I want us to live."

That was all I needed to hear. We proceeded to finalize everything with the owner and made plans for the payment. To be honest, the house was worth every bit of the $250,000 it was going to cost us. Tomorrow I would have my homeboy, who is a home inspector, come and check out the house to ensure there wasn't anything wrong with it and that nothing needed to be repaired.

The remainder of the day belonged solely to me and my Mrs.-to-be, and I had a surprise for her that she will undoubtedly love.

CHAPTER 19

Upon leaving the house we went downtown to have dinner at Mon Cheri's, a five-star restaurant located in the heart of the financial district. When we walked into the establishment, all eyes were on us as if to say, "what the hell were we doing in such a place?"

After we were seated by the hostess, a very attractive waitress approached our table and asked, "Good afternoon, how may I be of assistance to you today?"

I replied, "Well you could start by bringing us a bottle of your most expensive non-alcoholic wine." I knew I was in over my head, but practice makes perfect, and this was something I definitely needed to get used to.

She replied with a smile, "No problem, sir. Would you like to place your orders now or later?"

"Well actually, we're ready right now. Could you please bring us the shrimp scampi, mashed potatoes, garlic bread and salad, please? For desert, we would like to try your pineapple sundae."

"Will that be all, sir?"

"Yes, hmmmmm," I said looking at her name tag, trying to get her name. "Yes, Miss Facey. That will be all. Thank you very much."

"You are welcome. You two have a wonderful time here at Mon Cheri's," she replied, picking up the menus and walking towards the back to get our orders.

As soon as Ms. Facey walked away, Eve turned towards me and asked, "So Drew, when are we going to get married?"

Her question completely caught me off guard, in order to appease her I replied, "Whenever you're ready."

"Well, I wanted us to get married before the baby gets here in December, so I was thinking more like the end of November, before your finals come up."

"I think that's a good idea, babe. Plus, by then both our parents would have adjusted to the situation."

"Drew, I'm so excited. I'm about to have my own family and I've got the man of my dreams. What more could a girl ask for?"

I decided that this was the ideal moment, so I reached into my pocket, pulling out a 3 ½ carat diamond ring I'd purchased a couple days ago at Zales in Green Acres mall. Steering directly into her eyes, I knelt in front of her with the ring in hand and said, "I've been waiting for the perfect time to do this, so here goes. Eve, will you please take my hand in marriage?"

Tears were now rolling down her cheeks, slightly smudging the mascara she wore as she replied, "Yes baby, I will."

We now had the attention of the entire restaurant as all the patrons began clapping. I placed the ring on her finger, making sure to take my time so the moment could last a little while longer. After the ring was securely placed on her finger, I got up and embraced her to let her know how much I loved her. Seconds later, our waitress returned with our orders, smiling and said, "Congratulations on your engagement you two." Sharing in our special moment.

For the remainder of the evening, we enjoyed our meal as we made plans for the future we were about to share together, and discussed plans for our wedding and honeymoon. After we got finished eating, I motioned over our waitress and paid the tab, making sure to leave Ms. Facey a $50 tip, which had her in all smiles. On the way back to Eve's apartment, my cell phone started ringing, which startled me a bit. I was hoping it wasn't one of my jump-offs calling to nag me while I was out with her, because if that was the case, it was guaranteed that they wouldn't hear the end of it. When I glanced at the caller ID I realized it was Abdul calling me. I figured it had to be important because I made sure to give them specific instructions that I was not to be disturbed unless it was an emergency.

I answered, "Yo, what's good son?" I could tell immediately that something was wrong when he hesitated. Then he replied, "We've been hit, son. Kendu's, been shot and killed. I can't really say much right now, but I will break everything down when I see you."

"Aight, meet me at the spot in 2 hours."

"Aight one."

After hearing that Kendu was killed, I felt as if I'd just been stabbed in the chest by a 12inch steak knife. That shit just fucked up my entire mood. Eve was now looking at me with sheer concern on her face as she asked, "Baby, is everything alright?"

I replied, "Nah baby, one of my boys just got killed. I've got to go see what happened so I'm gonna drop you home and I'll come see you later on tonight.

"Ok baby, just please be careful and promise me you won't do nothing stupid. "

"Alright, babe. You don't have to worry about that, I promise."

CHAPTER 20

By the time I got to the stash house over on Guy R Brewer the entire crew was there, posted up in the living room with Clark pacing the floor. I walked in and greeted everyone then I sat with Abdul and Clark to see what was up.

I made sure to get right to the point as I turned to Abdul and asked, "Yow son, what the fuck happened?"

"Some dude name Killa over on Jamaica Ave killed him," he replied.

"How the hell did he get to him, and what was the motive?"

"Well, do you remember the dude we robbed and killed over on the Westside a couple weeks ago?"

"Yeah, why? What the hell does he have to do with this?

"Well, I found out that Killa is a distant cousin of his and they both were hustling together over the past couple years. To make a long story short, he somehow found out we were involved in his cousin's death and he's vowed to get us back, one by one."

"So how did he get the drop on Kendu?"

"Some chick named Tina, Kendu was messing with over on Foch Blvd called him up saying her cousin needed some work, so Kendu came and got it to head over there. When he pulled up to her house he didn't even get the chance to get out his car before son ran up on him, popping him in the head twice, robbing him of everything he had along with the work."

"How much work did he make off with?"

"A total of 7lbs of weed and 1000 pills."

This all didn't sound right to me. I could tell that something fishy had gone down and I had a strong feeling that bitch Tina, had something to do with Kendu's murder and I was determined to find out and avenge my comrade's death.

Directing my attention to Abdul I asked, "Yow, do you know where this chick lives at?"

He replied, "Yeah I do. Why do you want to know? Are you thinking what I'm thinking?"

"Only if you're thinking revenge," I said angrily.

"We would have made Kendu proud", he replied with a smile plastered on his face.

CHAPTER 21

Minutes later, we were in a crackhead's car, strapped heading to Tina's apartment to pay her a much needed visit.

When we pulled up to her place all the lights were out besides the one in the back of the house which I figured must have been her bedroom. A block away across the street, were crime scene tape were Kendu was murdered. Seeing this only infuriated me more and infused my thirst for revenge. Soon we made it out the car, one by one heading toward the back of the house trying to find our way in. To my surprise, the window leading to the kitchen was left halfway open, so I sent Abdul in being that he was skinniest out the crew. When he made it inside, he immediately went around to the back door to let Clark and myself in. Upon entering the apartment, we split up in an effort to secure the parameters in search of our prey. Clark and Abdul went on to check the bathroom and living room, while I proceeded to check the bedroom.

As I slowly approached the bedroom door, I heard a female's voice engulfed in laughter. The door was halfway open so I peaked in to see if she was alone. When I peered into the room, I saw a female whom I figured to be Tina, sitting in a bed full of money, laughing at a program on the T.V.

"I was gonna have fun watching her pay for snaking my boy", I thought to myself.

Gripping the rubber handle of my 9 mm, I walked into the bedroom, pointing the pistol directly at her, "You better not make a motherfucking sound", I stated with blood in my eye.

The look on her face said it all. Fear encompassed her as she sat speechless on the bed looking dumbfounded.

"So you really thought I wouldn't find out you the one that set up my boy huh, and look at you sitting here celebrating your accomplishment in selling him out. You dumb bitch".

Tears were now streaming down her cheeks as she whispered, "I swear this wasn't my idea. I truly cared about Kendu, I swear you gotta believe me. I was forced to do it".

Hearing her say his name only added fuel to the fire, leading me to pistol whip her twice in her face, causing her to bleed from the right side of her forehead.

"Bitch if you want to live a little bit longer you better get that fool Killa over here asap"

Within seconds both Clark and Abdul came running through the bedroom door asking, "Is everything aight in here?"

"Tina and I were just working on a mutual agreement on something that's all, but everything is good now, right Tina?"

She immediately shook her head in agreement. With all the strength she could muster, she reached for her phone as instructed, putting on the sexiest voice she could in an effort to get Killa to come pay her a visit.

When she made it off the phone, I snatched it from her, checking to ensure she didn't try any funny shit.

Upon the 3rd ring, the persons voicemail came on confirming that it was in fact Killa's number.

Within a few minutes, her phone started ringing, it was Killa calling her back. So I urged her to answer.

"Hello, yea I'll be here waiting on you. Ok see you soon", she responded to the person on the other line before ending the call.

When she got off the phone she looked at me and said, "He said he will be here in less that a minute, he is just a block away".

"Ight then, let's go" I stated ushering her toward the front door.

Upon making it to the living room, we positioned ourselves on both sides of the door, making it difficult for us to be seen.

Seconds later there was a knock at the door announcing the arrival of our guest of honor.

Using my free hand, I motioned Tina to open the door and not to make any funny moves when she did.

As the door swung open, Killa made his way inside, oblivious to what was awaiting him.

Seeing this as my only option to attack, I snuck up behind him, gun butting him in the head, knocking him out cold.

Redirecting my attention to Abdul and Clark I ordered; "Yo tie them both up, I got something real special in store for these pieces of shit".

In the mean time I made my way to the kitchen to find my weapon of choice. We all wore gloves to ensure there were no prints left at the scene to link us to what was about to happen. That was one less thing we had to worry about.

As I rummaged through the kitchen shelves, I saw something that caught my eye and that would be ideal.

Pulling out an 18-inch machete from under the kitchen sink, I caught a glimpse of my reflection on the metal blade. What I saw was the face of a deranged man out to quench his thirst for revenge.

After grabbing a few garbage bags, I made my way back to the living room to join the party.

By the time I made it to the living room, my boys already had Tina and Killa tied to each other and gagged to ensure they weren't able to make a sound during my torture session.

"Yo Abdul, Clark, here put these bags over your clothes so there won't be any blood splattered over your shit", I said handing them the garbage bags I retrieved from the kitchen.

I was determined to have both Tina and Killa suffer for what they did, and nothing would stop me from doing so.

Directing my attention towards them, I saw the fear in their eyes which put a smile on my face.

Walking over to Killa with the machete in hand I barked, "You really thought you could mess with us and get away it huh? you dumb piece a shit"

What I did next surprised everyone in the room as I raised the machete in the air, bringing it back down with brutal force, chopping away at both their bodies simultaneously, causing them to squirm in agony as blood gushed everywhere.

Pain and fear now became more prevalent on their faces which only caused my actions to become more intense. I continued on my rampage with no remorse dissecting their bodies immensely. Looking at the work I had just put in I could have easily been a good butcher.

Satisfied, I called over Clark and Abdul to help me clean up a bit, back tracking our movements so we could get the hell out a there.

While on our way out the house, we heard a knock at the front door which startled us.

"NYPD, open up, we've got some questions we need to ask you Ms Jones" Bam, Bam, Bam. "Open up".

That shit was all we needed to hear to know it was time to get the hell outta dodge.

As we made our exit through the back headed towards the car, I noticed two police cars parked in front the house, which caused us to make an immediate detour.

"Yo fellas, we gotta split up and try to make a run for it, fuck the car. More than likely they got cops on that block posted up so we gotta improvise. We will meet back up at the stash house on Highgate".

"Are you sure Drew", Abdul asked concerned.

"Yea bro, worst comes to worst, we gotta shoot our way out this shit. Ain't no way I'm going to jail. High Rollaz for life my dudes, no retreat no surrender".

As we began making our exit, we saw two uniformed officers heading our way guns drawn yelling; "Freeze motherfuckas".

One by one we pulled our guns aimed at them opening fire. Immediately I aimed for the officer closest to me hitting him once in the head causing him to fall to his untimely death.

His partner returned fire instantly hitting Clark twice in the chest causing his lifeless body to hit the pavement.

Turning to Abdul I yelled, "Let's get the hell outta here".

The other officer was relentless, determined to wipe us out for killing his partner; and we had to make it out a there asap unless it was a sure thing we would be surrounded by NYPD in no time.

I had to think of something and fast. There was only one way out, and it was now or never.

"Yo Abdul, on the count of three I want you to take off, no looking back. I got you. No matter what just keep going and meet me back at the spot". The cop was now taking cover so we had to move fast.

"Aight bro, love you man".

"Love you too brah. Get ready, 1, 2, 3, now".

As soon as Abdul got up from behind the car where we were previously taking cover, I aimed my pistol in the direction of the cop. Just as expected he rose from his hide out in hopes of getting a shot at Abdul.

Before he had the opportunity to do so, I squeezed the trigger once hitting him in the arm. The impact from the bullet caused him to hit the floor in excruciating pain.

Sensing this was my only chance at escaping, I immediately began running as fast as I could as sounds of sirens began getting farther and farther. Not even Usain Bolt could beat me at that point. I was determined not to get caught. It was a sure thing if I did, I would never see the light of day ever again.

CHAPTER 22

By the time I got to the apartment on Highgate, Abdul was already there, anxiously awaiting my arrival.

As I walked in the door, I spotted him in the dark sitting on the loveseat he had stationed in the living room with his gun drawn.

"Yo Drew, you know you are one crazy dude son. You had me scared shitless that something might have happened to you."

I replied, "I'm a big boy, Abdul. I know how to take care of myself. How are you holding up though?"

"I'm doing aight. It's just fucked up how we lost two good dudes over some bullshit in less than a day, but we can't stop now. We done came too far to give up now; there's no turning back."

"You're right, son. We've got to do this for Kendu and Clark."

"No doubt, Drew. You know I'm here for you a hundred percent."

"Aight, this is what I'm going to need you to do: I need you to hold down the fort for a couple of days, just so I could lay low for a little while. If you need me for anything just give me a call. If anyone asks for me just tell them I went out of town for a few days. I also need you to get one of your girls to contact both Kendu and Clark's parents notifying them about what happened and to send them each $20,000 to cover funeral costs."

"Aight son, you ain't got nothing to worry about, I got you."

"Oh, and Abdul before I forget, I will make sure to call D to let him know I won't be around for a couple of days, so if he contacts you for some work, just make the link."

"Aight bro, whatever it is I got you."

"Ay yo Abdul," I said, turning around facing him.

"What's up baby boy?"

"Please be careful, I can't afford to lose you also."

Walking up to me, Abdul embraced me and then replied, "I love you homie."

As I made it out front to my truck I grabbed my cell dialing Eve's phone number. It was already three in the morning but, I knew without a doubt that she would be waiting up for my phone call. On the second ring, she answered, "Hey baby, where are you? I've been worried sick!"

"I'm on my way right now. I'm truly sorry I didn't get the chance to call you before," I replied.

"Ok baby, I'll be waiting up for you."

"Ok Love, I'll see you in a little while. Oh, and Eve…"

"Yes, baby?"

"I love you."

With a light chuckle she replied, "I love you too" before hanging up.

By the time I made it to Eve's apartment, it was already going on four in the morning, and to my surprise she was still up, sitting by the bedroom window waiting for me. When I reached the front door, she was standing there wrapped in a silk robe with a look of concern on her face. I didn't even get to walk inside before I was interrogated, "Drew, what happened tonight?"

Looking at her with the utmost sincerity in my eyes I said, "It's a long story, baby. Right now, I just want to take a bath and go to bed. I promise I'll tell you everything in the morning, but right now, I need some rest."

"Ok baby, I'll go get your bath water ready," she replied and headed for the bathroom.

After a few minutes, I went into the bathroom. The first thing I noticed was the smell of incense burning, then I saw candles lit and positioned all around the bath tub with Eve laying completely nude in the tub, waiting for me to join her. This woman was definitely one of a kind. At times, I would find myself questioning whether or not I was good enough for her.

That night, we took turns bathing each other and making love over and over again until we both climaxed in ecstasy. The time we shared together was truly amazing and I was determined not to mess it up, but then again, I was also involved with Michelle, so I was stuck in a complicated situation of being in love with two different women who were about to be the mothers of my children.

CHAPTER 23

It was the one-month anniversary of Kendu and Clark's death and business had been booming in unexpected proportions. We were now bringing in revenue of $650,000 per week. Since the murders, the NYPD was on my back, trying to link me to the bodies, but no matter how hard they tried, they could not find any substantial evidence to do so. For all they knew, I was just a good college kid from an upper-class family with a wealthy fiancé. I had also finally built up the courage to break the news to my family that I was engaged to be married, and that they were about to be grandparents. At first, they didn't take the news very well as it was a complete shock to them, but in time they came around, with my mother making plans and preparations for the wedding. Even Eve's parents were making plans to come to the United States for the wedding.

I also introduced Michelle and Eve to each other for the first time. They had to have an amicable relationship, so why not start now. I must admit it was awkward having the two women I loved, the mothers of my children sitting in one room, knowing they were both pregnant with my babies. I knew they would have to meet each other sooner or later; I ended up choosing sooner. It took me a lot of explaining to Eve, to break down how the entire situation came about and I must say, it was the hardest two hours of my entire life. At one point I felt as if she was about to rip my head off, but after reassuring her that she was the love of my life and that Michelle had gotten pregnant way before we became serious, she relaxed a little and agreed to meet with her.

I was determined not to have any type of drama between the two, and this was the best way I figured we could go about the situation. All in all, everything went pretty smooth.

Today my mother was scheduled to fly in from Albany to meet with both Eve and Michelle. I already gave her the run down on them both, so she already knew what to expect. My father wanted to make it for the trip, but was unable to because he had some important business to take care of back home. Eve and I had already moved into our condo on Longmeadow and my mother would be staying with us for the weekend. Her plane was set to land within the next forty-five minutes; so we had to get going if we didn't want to have her waiting, which would be a bad idea.

"Let's go Eve. Don't worry, you look great. I'm positive my mother will love you."

"Are you sure baby? I'm not trying to mess up her first impression of me; you know the first impression is usually a lasting one."

"Baby, don't sweat it. You're good to go."

I must admit, Eve was looking stunning in her off-white Louis Vuitton pants suit with the matching open-toe heels. I had to fight the urge to get a quick taste of her loving before we left, because I knew if I was ever late to pick up my mother, I wouldn't hear the end of it.

"Ok, let's go baby."

"Go on and start the car Drew, I'll be out in a minute. I just gotta lock up."

"Alright then, just make sure to hurry."

When I went outside and hopped in my truck, I had to pause for a while to get my thoughts together. I knew for a fact that my mother would be asking personal questions about my life; I had to find a way to evade them for most of her trip. Seconds later, Eve opened the door and hopped in the car, jarring me from my thoughts. I turned to her and said, "Baby, no matter what happens, I'm going to need you to go along with everything I say to my mother, and I'll make sure to do the same for you."

With a smile she replied, "I'm here for you, no matter what. You're my man and my king."

That statement definitely put a smile on my face as I leaned over towards her, planting a kiss on her lips.

CHAPTER 24

By the time we pulled up to the arrival ramp at American Airlines, I saw my mother exiting the building, looking beautiful as always. It was definitely not hard to tell where I got my looks; even at forty-four years old, my mother was still a very attractive woman. She was 5ft 5inches tall, caramel complexion, with shoulder-length hair and she weighed about 130 lbs. The first thing that caught my eye was the two enormous bags she had in tow. She was only going to be in town for a couple of days, but by the look of her bags, you would get the impression she was spending a month or so. She was a true shopaholic and there was no doubt in my mind she would get along pretty well with Eve.

When I pulled up to the curb I hopped out the truck, running over to my mother with open arms, embracing her. "Hey ma, how was your flight?"

"It was ok baby. Look at you, you've lost a lot of weight since I last saw you, but don't worry, mommy is here to take care of all that."

Just then, Eve came out of the car, walking over to us to greet my mother. Extending her hand she said, "How are you doing, Mrs. Brown?"

"Baby, come here and give me a hug. Your family now so you can just call me Catherine." Redirecting her attention towards me she said. "Drew, you didn't tell me she was this beautiful. Oh and darling," she said to Eve, "I absolutely love that outfit; we've definitely got to go shopping."

Eve was now all smiles, I could tell by her expression that she was more than satisfied with her first impression.

"Ok mom, let's get going."

Before she got in the car she asked, "Baby, whose truck is this?"

"It's mines, Ma," I replied hoping she would leave it at that.

"Drew, where did you get money to pay for this? And what happened to your Maxima?"

"Well, the truck was a gift from Eve and we ended up using the Maxima as a trade-in."

I knew for a fact that I hadn't heard the last of her interrogation. I had to do whatever possible not to be alone with her over the course of the weekend, starting right now.

"Hey, Ma, why don't you and Eve sit together in the back and enjoy the ride? I'm sure you have a lot to talk about."

With a light smile, she replied, "Ok son, that's a great idea. I'm sure I could learn a couple things from Eve about fashion, and vice versa.

I knew that what I'd done, putting Eve on the spot like that, was messed up, but better her than me. She would need to get used to my Mother anyways, so now is as good a time as any.

"So, Ma, what do you have planned for the day?"

"Today, my time is solely dedicated to getting to know Eve and Michelle, so we're going shopping and then to dinner."

"That sounds like a good idea to me. What about you Eve?"

"I'm definitely looking forward to it," she replied.

Taking a quick second to look back at her facial expression, I could tell she was lying through her teeth, but I must admit it was amusing seeing her in such a compromising position. I just knew I was in store for a mean tongue lashing after all this. It was a good thing that they wouldn't need me for the remainder of the day because I had some important business I needed to tend to, and with them going out, I had the perfect opportunity to do so.

When we got to the apartment, I dropped them off and left immediately after, heading to D's office downtown to meet with him and his financial planner. I needed to find a legit way to go about washing my money and at the same time multiply it, so I decided to invest my money in some sort of business; and who better to guide me in doing so than D. I was about five minutes away from his office when I decided to give him a call letting him know I was on my way.

Ring, Ring, Ring.

"Good afternoon, business offices of Davis and Washington, Shannon speaking. How may I help you?"

"What's going on Shannon? It's me, Drew."

"Oh, hey Drew, how're you doing today?"

"I'm doing ok, and you?"

"I'm great."

"That's good to hear. Sweetheart, would you please let Mr. Davis know that I'll be there in the next couple of minutes?"

"I sure will, Drew. I do believe he's in his office waiting on you, so I'll make sure he receives the message."

"Great, I'll see you soon."

"Take care."

Shannon was definitely a sweetheart and a cutie. She was quite petite at 5ft 2inches, 110 lbs. with a banging body, half-Japanese with hair down her back. From time to time, D would tell me stories of how good she was in bed and how her head game was out of this world, and to be honest, hearing this only peaked my interest more and more. I just knew I would be finding out all this sometime soon, but I just had to choose the right time to do so. The moment I pulled up to the front of the office building, I saw D outside smoking a cigar talking to a much older-looking white dude whom I presumed to be his financial planner. When I approached them, D greeted me with a hug and introduced the gentleman to me as a Mr. Polwinski. Extending my hand, I greeted him and said, "How are you doing, Mr. P?" I didn't know how to pronounce his last name and I didn't want to come off as ignorant, so I opted to use 'Mr. P'.

"I'm doing pretty well, Mr. Brown," he replied, extending his hand as we locked into a firm handshake.

D then said, "Well guys, let's go to my office so we can get down to business."

"That sounds like a good idea," I replied, making my way to the front entrance with D and Mr. P in tow.

Within minutes, we were all seated at a round table in D's office with one thing in mind, which was making money.

Directing his attention to me D said, "Drew, Mr. P is the absolute best at what he does and he is the man who has helped me to get where I am at this moment. I already gave him the rundown of your situation, so for most part he already knows what he is dealing with."

"Aight D, good looking out. So Mr. P, what can I do for you and vice versa?"

"Well Mr. Brown, let me start by asking you this: do you by any chance like clubbing?"

"Of course I do, Mr. P. Why, what's up?"

"Well I feel it would be beneficial for you to invest in a night club. You could lease a building for a year, ranging in price anywhere from $50,000 to $100,000. Now, this is where it all gets better. You could end up renting out the club to your friends at relatively low prices, but on paper you would have to boost up the cost to cover your ass; and at the same time, you can throw parties charging let's say up to $5 but on the flyer, the admission would range anywhere from $10-$20."

"Mr. P, your proposal sounds irresistible, but before we go any further, where would I find a club owner willing to lease us their nightclub?"

"You don't have to worry about that, Mr. Brown. That is what I was hired for. All I need from you is the go ahead and I'll have everything ready to take off by the end of this week."

"Well, I must admit Mr. P, it seems like you know what you're talking about. What do you think, D?"

"It sounds good to me, Drew, but it's your call."

I then turned to Mr. P and said, "You have my permission to proceed, just give me a buzz and let me know when and where to meet you to finalize everything."

"OK, Mr. Brown, I'll make sure to keep you posted."

We then shook hands, sealing our agreement before I made my way out of the office.

CHAPTER 25

On my way out the building I accidentally bumped into Shannon, almost knocking her to the floor.

"Oh, pardon me Drew"

"No, excuse me. I almost killed you there", I replied with a smirk.

"That's ok, it's partly my fault anyways for not looking where I was going."

"What are you about to do", I asked.

"Well I am about to finish up this proposal for Mr. Davis before I leave. Why do you need something done?"

Deep down I wanted to say, 'Yes, I want to fuck your brains out'; but I had to refrain myself from doing so and possibly making a fool of myself. Instead I opted to say, "I am heading in your direction so was checking to see if you would like a ride home".

Without hesitation, she smiled and said, "That would be great Drew, just give me a few minutes to finish up."

"Aight, I'll be waiting for you out front."

On the way to my car I became struck by guilt, thinking to myself; "Drew you know better than to venture off into those waters, just take her home and leave. You owe that much to Eve."

Within minutes there was a knock at my window, startling me. When I looked up to see who it was I saw Shannon standing there with a cool aid smile plastered across her face asking; "Are you ready to go Drew?", gently biting on her bottom lip.

Hearing those words roll off her tongue causing my manhood to stand at attention. I immediately reached for my jacket, placing it over my lap trying to conceal the bulge, but came up unsuccessful in doing so.

Upon making her way into the passenger seat, Shannon began smiling at the bulge protruding through my pants.

"Do you need some help releasing some of that tension big boy?", she teased licking her lips.

Before I was able to answer, she reached for my pants, unfastening my belt, pulling down my zipper; making way for the entrance of my dick inside her warm mouth.

The sensation I received from her French kissing my love muscle was definitely mind blowing, but at the same time I felt guilty indulging in such an act, knowing I had a loving woman at home, but my thirst for pleasure quickly overshadowed the guilt.

As if a sign from up above my phone started to ring. By the ringtone I knew it was Eve calling so I answered.

"Hey baby, where are you?", I asked pulling Shannon's head from my lap I motioned to her to be quiet.

"We are home baby. I was calling to let you know that everything went great today. Also, we are having a cookout tomorrow so make sure to invite your friends; and try to get your boy Maine to come through and Dj."

"Ok sweetie, that's good to hear that you all had fun today. Where is my Mother?"

"She is laying down at the moment. Oh, and baby, will you be making it home soon? I miss you."

"I'm honestly not sure, but I will try my best, I still got a few things I need to take care of."

Okay, see you soon"

As I made it off the phone, I turned to Shannon and said, "I'm truly sorry, but I can't do this right now. It has nothing to do with you, but I just can't.

"Don't worry about it Drew, I understand, there is no love lost here", she replied leaning over to plant a kiss on my cheek.

I then pulled my zipper up and fastened my belt, before pulling away from the curb on the way to drop her home. I knew I needed to do better and be faithful to the love of my life. This was just the first step in doing so.

CHAPTER 26

After dropping Shannon home, I headed over to my old apartment to spend a little time with my old house mates. When I got there Maine and Chris were just pulling into the drive way.

While greeting each other I could sense there was a little uneasiness between us. This was mainly due to the fact I wasn't spending time with them like I used to. After moving out a month ago; this was my first visit since. I was however positive that once we all hooked up, all that uneasiness will fly out the window. As expected all that was needed was a couple spliffs and some video games and we would be back to the old days. Maine was busy on the turn tables doing what he does best and Chris and I was busy playing Madden as usual. I must admit it felt good sitting there chillin with friends, having fun without a care in the world. We sat there for hours on end bullshitting, getting high and cracking jokes like there was no tomorrow. If it was up to me I would have stayed the entire night, but I had a family I needed to make it home to, I had a lot of care in the world; and I enjoyed it. For once, things were looking great again, and my two lost soldiers will forever be in my thoughts. As long as I'm good, their family and kids are good also. Kendu had a 2-year-old and after Clark's death we came to find out his girlfriend was pregnant.

It was getting late and definitely time to go.

On my way out the door, it dawned on me to tell the fellas to pass through at the cookout and let Maine know I would need him to play, so he would need to bring his equipment Pausing my exit I turned to them and said,"Yo fellas, we having a cookout at my place tomorrow, so make sure y'all pass by around noon and walk with your empty stomachs. Oh and Maine, I'm a need you to Dj, so bring your equipment with you.

Aight Drew, you know I got you. I'll pass through before 12 to set up", Maine said with a light smile.

Before walking through the door, I reached into my pocket, pulling out a wad of cash giving them a thousand a piece.

"What's this for bro?" Maine asked dumbfoundedly.

"That's just a little something for y'all, enjoy it". Real dudes do real things, and you guys have always kept it real with me."

"Aight bro, one love", they relied in unison.

"No doubt, and make sure I see y'all fools tomorrow, and come on you're A game. Some a Eve's fly ass friends gonna be there along with Michelle's house mates. And trust, they all wanna be chosen", I said laughing on my way out the door.

CHAPTER 27

After leaving my old apartment I was finally on my way home, hoping to make it to my baby before she fell asleep. But upon my arrival, it was evident I was too late. All the lights were off besides the ones surrounding the house and in the hallway.

The very first thing I did was to head to the guestroom to check on my Mom. To my surprise she was peacefully asleep. She must a been exhausted, because generally she would wait up until I get home.

When I made it down the hall to the master bedroom, I saw my Eve passed out sleeping while Seinfield re-runs sat and watched her. For some dam reason she could never get enough of Cosmo Kramer.

I reached for the remote to turn off the T.V, then planted a kiss on her forehead while tucking her in.

Upon feeling the warmth of my kiss, she opened her eyes and smiled; and it felt natural for me to do the same. I was really in love with this woman and I for sure could get use to waking up to her face every morning.

That night we laid in each other arms, and dreamt of the future and our perfect realities of it.

CHAPTER 28

The following morning, I woke up to the sweet aroma of my Mother's mouth watering disses. She gave true meaning to Yard Style Kitchen. Being of Jamaican decent, she always knew how to throw down in the kitchen, and nobody ever tops her Oxtail with butter beans or her Stew Peas.

Checking my watch for the time it read 1:30 pm, which caused me to get my black ass outta bed. I wasn't tryna be a party pooper and sleep out the entire event.

After I got out the shower, I was headed to the closet to find something to wear. Upon opening the closet, I saw my baby had picked out for me a lavender colored Christian Dior Linen shorts along with the shirt to match and a pair of white Pradas.

Seconds later I heard a knock at my bedroom door so I questioned, "Who is it?"

"Drew, it's me Michelle, your mother sent me to check up on you".

I must admit, hearing Michelle's voice definitely put a smile on my face.

"Come on in, I'm just about finished getting ready".

Michelle looked gorgeous as always, even with her baby bump. I know exactly what my mother was trying to accomplish; and I must admit it would have worked any other time, but I just couldn't risk what I had with Eve for no one.

With a warm smile I said, "It's good to see you could make it, you look absolutely beautiful I might add".

"And you don't look too bad yourself Sir", she responded smiling ear to ear.

We both share a hearty laugh before momentarily exiting the bedroom to go join the party.

The backyard was filled with at least 30 individuals having fun and enjoying great food. What started out as a cook out was now a full-blown house party.

Peering through the crowd, I spotted a few familiar faces. All my old house mates were there. D and some friends were chillin by the pool with some of Michelle's trifling house mates; while Abdul and a few dudes from my team were conversing with some attractive females I presumed to be Eve's home girls.

"Over hear Drew", I heard my Mother yell. Directing my attention to the sound of her voice, I located her on the patio with Eve, sitting across from Eric and a very attractive white woman. I have always been pro black when it came to dating until I met Eve, and trust me this woman would have me thinking of venturing into the snow just the same, if I wasn't partially married; I thought to myself smiling.

Making my way onto the patio I asked, "What are you all here getting into?"

"Just here getting acquainted with Eric and his lady friend. Isn't she pretty?" my Mom said as always being my Mother doing a great job at providing the ideal ice breaker.

While greeting everyone, I came to find out Liz, Eric's date is actually a Drug Enforcement Agent. There is no wonder how he was able to run his distribution so smooth. That inside link always does the trick.

"Shall we eat?", my Moms asked, making her way over to the lawn table filled with food, with everyone including me in tow.

What I saw on that table put a smile on my face immediately. The was curried goat, oxtail, jerk chicken, rice and peas with friend plantains. Along with baked Mac and Cheese and my favorite, rum cake with frosting.

Everyone took turns getting their plates filled and even returning for seconds and thirds. Mom dukes for sure put her foot in this one.

The night ended on a high note and everyone went home smiling.

Before retreating to bed, I went to tell her good night. 'Knock, knock'.

"Whose there?", she said jokingly. "Come here baby, I wanna talk to you before I go to bed".

As always, I was due a pep talk, our mother son ritual.

"Baby, I'm a make this short. You are blessed with two lovely women in your life to be the mothers of your children. Cherish them, what's done is done. It's now time for you to man up and be the person you know how to be, and hurry up and get married to the mamcita, she is a doll", my Mother said smiling from ear to ear.

Thanks a lot for being honest with me and I definitely see where you are coming from. I just feel as if I am stuck in a messed-up predicament because I love both these women with all my heart, but at the same time I had to make a choice, I just hope I haven't made the wrong one.

Well baby you have from now until November to finalize that decision, but no matter what your decision is your father and I will always be here to support you.

That is something you don't ever have to worry about baby, and that's a promise.

Leaning forward I embraced her, planting a kiss on my queens' cheek and whispered, "sleep tight mom, I'll see you in the morning."

"Ok baby, just think about what I said."

"I promise you I will Ma", I said as I made my way out the room.

Upon entering my bedroom, I noticed pieces of clothing laying on the carpet forming a trail from the bed to the bathroom.

Being an obedient young man, I stripped naked making a hastily retreat to the bathroom to go join my boo.

In the Jacuzzi, I saw Eve naked as the day she was born with her perky breast glistening beneath the water; laying in the tub while scented candles burned, illuminating the bathroom.

Looking towards her I said; "I see you went ahead and prepped for the after party?"

"I'm only getting ready for you love", she replied with a devilish grin on her face.

Eager to soothe my yearning for her I made my way into the tub. We then took turns bathing each other ensuring there wasn't a body part left neglected.

After we got done I climbed out the Jacuzzi anticipating all that would ensue. Placing my hands beneath her body, I removed her from the jacuzzi, laying her on the plush Egyptian carpet that encompassed the bathroom floor.

Running my hands over her breasts, I lingered on her nipples. Looking into her eyes I could tell she wanted me to continue so I did. Using my tongue, I began to slowly massage her entire body, starting at her neck and making my way down to her vagina, slowly teasing it with every taste.

She was now squirming with pleasure, but being the freak she is, she had to have me in her mouth.

Elevating her back off the carpet, she leaned forward in front my fat love muscle and slowly took me in her mouth causing my dick to stand at full attention, anticipating what was to come.

She made love to my dick with the wetness of her mouth, while enjoying the look on my face as I squirmed from pleasure. Using my fingers to penetrate her, I searched relentlessly in the quest to locate her g spot.

I wanted to taste her, but getting head felt so damn good I didn't want her to stop, I wanted it all.

Momentarily pulling my fingers out I placed them on the tip of my tongue, tasting the sweetness of her juices, which only intensified the urge and need to quench my thirst.

"lay down baby, "I whispered and she complied with urgency.

As she lay there on the carpet all I could think about was her cumin on the tip of my tongue. Lowering my face between her legs I placed my tongue on her clit, slowly moving it up and down massaging it with each stroke.

I could tell what I was doing worked like a charm by the way her body began to twitch. Seconds later she had her legs over my shoulders and her nails slowly penetrating my skin. That shit turned me on even more, causing me to slide a finger inside her pussy while licking her clit.

"Dddddreeww I I I'm Cumm mm in", she was unable to get that last word out, I felt her body begin to shake uncontrollably as she tried relentlessly to push my head away.

Eager to make this climax one to remember I remained where I was continuing to gently suck on her clit until I felt like she had enough.

Pulling me closer to her, Eve reached for my throbbing dick, knowing exactly what I needed.

Using her free hand, she slowing guided my dick into her place of pleasure. As I entered her vagina, the wetness engulfed me, while I made continuous winding motions inside her gently sucking on her breasts simultaneously. I wanted to cum and I could tell she wanted me to also.

"Cum inside your pussy papi", Eve whispered in my ear as she thrusted forward to meet my motions.

I couldn't hold back any longer, the tip of my dick started to tingle and my hips began to twitch. I'm cumin baby, oh fuck" I yelled. To my surprise Eve was also on the verge of climaxing, so she edged me on.

"This is your pussy papi, fill me up"

We both erupted at the same time and that shit felt like a taste of heaven.

I could definitely see myself getting use to this.

CHAPTER 29

The cool summer breeze hit me as I made my exit from La Guardia international airport, moments later after dropping off my old lady.

That woman is definitely one of a kind and I must admit I was missing her already.

I had a lot of things I needed to take care of today, but first up was to get in contact with Mr. Polwinski to set up a time to finalize our little transaction.

On my way over to the stash house on Minnesota I dialed his number.

Ring, ring, ring, ring

After the fourth ring, a familiar voice answered and said; "Hello, who is this?"

"This is Mr. Brown, is Mr. Polwinski available?"

"Oh, hi Drew, what can I do for you"?"

"That's what I am trying to figure out myself Mr. P".

"Did D relay the message to you?"

"Yea he did"

"So how does everything sound to you?", he asked.

"If everything is as he said, I am down for it 100 percent. As a matter a fact I am on my way to get the money as we speak, so I was calling to see when and where would be suitable for us to meet up.

"Don't forget about what we are dealing with here Mr. Brown".

I must admit, his comment had me feeling a little uneasy as if something was up, but then I could always be wrong.

"Ok Mr. P, ten o clock at your office it is".

"I will make sure to have the paper work and everything ready for you, the only thing I will need is your John Hancock", he stated with a light chuckle.

"Alright Mr. P, I'll see you then."

As soon as I got off the phone, I went straight to the stash house to get the money before heading home.

Minutes later a call came in from Michelle, I answered right away.

"What's going on hun, everything ok?", I asked.

"Drew, where are you?"

By the tone of her voice I could tell that something was wrong, but I was unable to pinpoint what it was.

"I'm on Bailey Ave right now heading home, why what's good, are you ok?", I asked eager to find out what was up.

"Yea I am ok, right now I am just stranded at my girlfriend's apartment over on Breckenridge and Grant, so I need you to pick me up asap."

"I'm on my way, just hold tight."

"Ok, see you soon Drew, I love you"

"Love you too Mich", I stated before ending the call.

The sound of her voice left chills down my spine. This was definitely unlike her to leave home and be alone in her current state, much less to not have her car. Sensing that something was fishy, I called up Abdul telling him to meet me at the address, just in case it was a set up. A drive that would normally take 20 minutes took me only 10. My adrenaline was pumping at rapid speed and I was scared at the same time. Scared that something might be wrong, but hoping and praying that wasn't the case. Upon pulling up to the front of the house I tried relentlessly to reach Michelle but was unsuccessful in doing so. After the fifth attempt, I decided to walk to the entrance and ring the doorbell. After the first buzz, I came to realization that the front door was left partially open, so I knocked a few times calling out her name but was met with silence.

Reaching into my waist I pulled out my 40 Cal, removing the safety and intensified my grip on the handle while sweat trickled down the sides of my face.

As I entered the apartment with pistol in hand I could tell it was abandoned by the garbage and graffiti all over the walls.

It appeared the fear I had was in fact real, something had gone wrong and it doesn't seem pretty.

Eager to find her I began yelling, "Michelle, Michelle, where are you?" "Baby where are you, it's me Drew".

Making my way to what looked to be the remains of a kitchen, I heard sounds of rustling, as if something or someone was moving. "I hope that's her, I thought to myself" as I rushed inside.

The very moment I entered the kitchen what I say was my worst fear staring at me, which in turn caused me to fall to my knees wailing in tears. Michelle's lifeless body was tied to a chair in the middle of the kitchen with her stomach cut open and something that looked to be a baby's fetus lodged in her mouth.

All of a sudden, I heard a voice behind me say; "This is from D"

Within a split second I heard a gun go off. What I felt next was a burning sensation of lead piercing through my back and arm before fading to black.

CHAPTER 30

Three weeks later I woke up feeling groggy inside a hospital room with Eve by my side. My body was aching profusely, it felt as if I was being poked all over my body with needles. Surveying the room, I saw countless get-well cards and balloons with a bouquet of flowers on the night table at my bed side.

I was feeling a little weak and disoriented, but I was determined to find out what the hell happened and I needed to find out right now. With all the strength I was able to muster I tried easing my way up off the bed to get Eve's attention, but the more I tried the more my body ached. So, I opted to call her instead.

"Babe, Babe", I uttered trying to get her attention.

At that moment she opened her eyes with a smile plastered on her face as she got up out the chair, making her way over to me.

"Hey baby, how do you feel? I missed you so much"

Willing myself to speak some more I replied; "I'm ok, my body just aches a little".

"Just take it easy and relax baby, everything will be fine", she said planting a kiss on my lips.

"What really happened, and why am I in the hospital?" I asked wanting to be in the know.

"Oh baby, you don't remember anything do you?"

"Nah love, I have not the slightest idea".

Tears immediately began falling down her cheeks as she held my hand and said, "you were shot twice, once in your right arm and once in your back. Abdul found you at an abandoned house over on the west side, shot and left for dead. You have been in a coma for the past three weeks. So that is why you are unable to recall what happened".

I immediately began having flashbacks of what went down on that day, and the first thing that came to mind was the fact that I went to that house for the sole purpose of getting Michelle.

"So, I asked with urgency; "Baby where is Michelle?"

She immediately began shaking and the tears now started flowing freely. My intuitions indicated that something went horribly wrong.

"I'm sorry to have to tell you this baby, but Michelle is dead".

Instantaneously I felt as if my entire world just came crashing down on me. I could not hold back the tears that followed. I began whaling in agony and at the same time I started having cold sweats.

"She was found dead at the house with her stomach cut open and the fetus in her mouth"

Pain and revenge overwhelmed my body. "Why did they have to kill her, she didn't do anything to deserve this, and my poor baby didn't even get a chance at life. Eve and I sat in that hospital room consoling each other as we cried our eyes out mourning our loss. At that particular moment I made a vow that whoever committed these acts would pay dearly for it. Minutes later there was a knock at the door as two plain clothes officers entered the room. One looked to be somewhere in his late 50's while the other was probably in his 20's, so I figured he was the rookie being showed the ropes by the veteran.

The older officer then made his way over to me saying, "How are you holding up Mr. Brown? my name is detective Jones and this here is my partner detective Rollings"

With a stern look on my face I asked "What can I do for you guys?"

Detective Jones answered and said "No need to be alarmed Mr. Brown, we are just here to ask you a few questions and to try to figure out who is responsible for the murders and who tried killing you"

"Excuse me detective, but couldn't this wait until another time. As you can see my husband just woke up from a coma and is still recovering from his gunshot wounds", Eve stated sounding extremely annoyed.

I'm afraid not Mrs. Brown, whomever it was that committed these vile acts need to be taken off the streets as soon as possible, and I promise you this much, it won't be much longer and that's why we need your husband's assistance", replied detective Rollings.

Becoming agitated by the situation I said; "Let's get over with it, what do you want to know?"

Detective Jones then reached into his jacket pocket pulling out a notepad; "Do you know who tried killing you Mr. Brown?"

"I'm afraid I do not know that detective".

"Ok, so do you know anyone who would have wanted to kill you or Michelle for that matter?"

"No, I do not; I wish I could be of some kind of help to you detective, I really do but I would love to get the answers to those same questions as badly as you do"

"Is that so Mr. Brown? well I just have a few more questions for you then we will be on our way. I can see that we aren't getting anywhere with this".

"I thought you would have never realized that" I replied with a smirk on my face.

I could tell he was annoyed by my last comment by the way he folded his arms and shook his head.

"Are you still enrolled in school"

"Yes, I am and what does that have to do with anything?"

"Nothing in particular, I just wanted to know. Were you involved in any kind of illegal activities that would have caused you to have enemies, or any outstanding debts or anything of that nature?"

"No, I don't owe anyone anything and no I am not involved in anything illegal. Now will that be all detective? I am seriously starting to get a headache from all these questions"

"Well I have one last question to ask, but this is for your wife, Mrs. Brown did you and Michelle have a good relationship, and when was the last time you saw her?"

His last statement pissed me off to the point where I felt like getting up off my bed and kicking his ass. With pure fury in my eyes I stared at them and demanded they get the hell out.

Detective Jones then said, "I am truly sorry for my partners rudeness Mr. and Mrs. Brown, but please take my card and if anything comes to mind, please give me a call. The last thing I would want is to find out something happened to either of you and I could have done something to prevent it".

"Ok detective, just make sure to keep your dog on a leash next time"

"I'm truly sorry about this Mr. Brown, I can only imagine what you two are going through. Just take care of yourself and I do hope you recover soon" detective Jones said before he made his exit. Detective Rollings' question to Eve lingered in the back of my mind.

What if Eve was the one that wanted Michelle out the picture? But as soon as it popped into my head, I ruled it out immediately. There was no way Eve could have or would have done anything of that proportion.

CHAPTER 31

For the next couple of days Eve remained by my side faithfully, helping the medical staff along the way with whatever they needed, even helping me through my therapy sessions to nurse me back to recovery. At my request, I only wanted immediate family knowing that I was out of the coma, there was no telling who wanted me dead and I wanted to remain on the safe side by keeping my progress real discrete.

My memory was gradually coming back to me, and from time to time I would get flashbacks of the incident. I figured in time it would all come back full circle. Besides my memory being back fully, I was good to go. My doctor had scheduled for my release tomorrow morning and I was eager to be out of the hospital and home with my baby.

I had a ton of things I needed to take care of and one of those was to go visit Michelle and the baby at their gravesite. The more I thought about it, the more my heart became cold, yearning to avenge their deaths.

As far as business was concerned, D and Abdul were in charge of everything while I was out of commission, so I wasn't worried about that at all.

For the remainder of the evening, Eve and I just sat in bed talking about old times, reminiscing together before I drifted off to sleep, anticipating my release in the morning.

There she was in the middle of the kitchen with blood all over her body, and our baby's fetus hanging outside her mouth. All of a sudden, I heard someone behind me say, "Drew, this is from D". Giving way to the sound of gunshots.

I woke up immediately drenched in cold sweats sitting up in bed, looking around the hospital room to see if I was still dreaming. My entire body was now drenched with perspiration. When I looked over at the clock on the wall, the time read 2:30am. I was now forced to face the reality that my own man, the person who I looked up to, trusted and would have given my life for had in fact betrayed me.

Reaching for my phone on the nightstand I dialed. There was only one person I could depend on in a time like this, and I needed him now more than ever.

On the third ring, a familiar voice answered; "Yo, who is this?"

"Abdul, it's me Drew. Where you at right now?"

"Oh shit, what's up my dude, it's for sure good to hear your voice homie"

"I miss you too, but let's cut the reunion for later. No matter what no one is to know that I contacted you, especially not D".

"For sure Drew, what's popping though?"

"I can't say much right now, but meet me at my crib tomorrow afternoon around 2pm, and make sure to come alone and trust no one".

"For sure, I got you", he replied understanding instantly the importance of what I was saying.

"Aight my G, stay up"

"See you soon baby boy".

For the rest of the night I laid there in bed plotting my next move, trying to figure out how I would go about avenging Michelle and my baby's death, until I fell asleep.

That afternoon I woke up to Eve sitting next to me looking beautiful as ever. I was eager to get out of this hell hole and anxious to carry out my plot for revenge.

Directing my attention to Eve I asked, "Baby, how long have you been here?"

"Only about thirty minutes or so. You looked so peaceful sleeping, I didn't want to wake you up"

"I can't wait to get the help up out of here, so I can spend some quality time with my baby", a said with a light smile.

"Okay hun, let me go get the doctor so he can sign your release papers. I picked up some clothes for you to wear home, they are to your right on the night stand", she said pointed at a navy blue adidas sweat suit.

"Thanks baby, I have a few stops to make on our way home, so try to make it quick", I said with a smile while Eve made her exit.

By the time she made it back to the room with the doctor in tow, I was already fully dressed and waiting to leave.

With a smile on her face my doctor said, "Mr. Brown, I see that you are all set and ready to go. By the looks of everything you are well enough to be released, the only thing I ask of you Mr. Brown is to not strain yourself in any way by lifting or doing any kind a strenuous exercise".

"Not to worry doc, I got that covered", Eve said smiling. I'm sure the only strenuous exercise she had in mind was working my dick. It has been so long, I wonder if I would be able to satisfy her like I use to. "I promise I'll be gentle with him doc" Eve said causing us all to erupt in laughter.

On her way out the door Dr Davidson smiled and said, "You two take care and try not to have too much fun; and please stay out of trouble Mr. Brown".

Eager to get going I uttered, "Will do Doc, will do".

When we left the hospital, the first stop I had to make was to a flower shop, where I picked up two dozen white roses. Afterwards we hopped back into Eve's navy-blue Mercedes Benz headed to St Mathews cemetery over on Seneca street.

Upon arrival I asked Eve to give me a few minutes so I could pay my last respects to Michelle and our baby. At first, she was kind a hesitant to allow me to go alone, but after a little reassurance that I would be ok, she finally agreed to it.

As I made my way over to the gravesites I immediately became overwhelmed with emotion as tears began streaming down my cheeks. No matter how hard I tried, I could not hold back the tears any longer.

At first glance I saw a tombstone marked MICHELLE ANDRESON in bold letters, but what I saw next caused me to fall to my knees in pure agony. Next to Michelle's stone was a tombstone marked ALICIA BROWN, indicating that I would have had a baby girl, something I was completely unaware of until now.

For the next couple minutes, I knelt there weeping uncontrollably, blaming myself for my loved one's untimely death.

As I placed the roses on both their tombstones I made a vow to them that I would avenge their deaths; even if it was the last thing I did. Whoever was involved in their demise would pay dearly.

When I made it back to the car and peered into Eve's eyes, all I could see was sorrow, as tears streamed down her cheeks.

"I'm truly sorry any of this ever happened baby, and I just want to let you know that I will always be here for you no matter what" Ever uttered in a sincere tone.

For the next couple minutes, we sat parked inside the car holding each other as we both cried, unleashing our emotions.

This was the very first time I have ever cried so openly in anyone's presence and lord knows I tried not to; but that moment we shared at the cemetery only brought us closer together and solidified our relationship even more.

CHAPTER 32

On the way home from St. Mathews, I called up Abdul letting him know that I was on my way, in case he was already there waiting. He reassured me he was only a block away but to take my time. As expected, upon pulling into the drive way I saw Abdul's car parked alongside the curb. I immediately motioned him to come inside the house so we could discuss what we needed to in private.

"You looking good baby boy", Abdul stated giving me a dap. Getting down to business immediately he asked, "What's going on my dude, what's on your mind?"

Eager to get my plan underway I replied, "I know who is responsible for the shootings"

I could tell my response peaked his interest to the fullest as he leaned forward and asked, "Who did this shit?"

"Well to answer your question, the piece a shit responsible for all this is D, the person I thought was down for me all along, was the main person praying for my downfall", saying his name only infuriated me more.

"Drew, you sure about this?"

"Yea, I'm positive. Before getting shot I heard someone's voice behind me utter the words, "This is from D. So, I am positive. It's just crazy the way money changes or brings the true colors out someone, especially one you trust".

"That's my word, I should have known that two timing bastard was behind all this shit", Abdul stated while pacing around angrily.

"Why do you say that?" I asked curious.

"Well ever since the incident, he has been acting rather edgy around me, plus he has even offered to buy me out just in case you didn't pull through. All the signs were there, I was just being naïve thinking he probably was shook up about what happened. But it's now apparent he was acting this way solely because he was guilty of betrayal".

All I could picture in my head was making D pay for this shit. I was determined he would not live to see another day.

"Come to think of it, this chick I am seeing on the side told me recently that her baby father; some dude name Jo Jo who is one of D's gunners have been staying home a lot recently, constantly telling her he is just laying low for a little bit. I don't know why it took me so long to put two and two together. But trust me when I tell you this, those sons a bitches deserve whatever they got coming to them".

"Not to worry, I got a plan. I need you to call up D and tell him Eric called an emergency meeting with the both of you at the warehouse on Sycamore; and make sure to stress the fact that he wants you guys to come alone. Also round up Papa Smurf and Shizzle and snatch up that fool Jo Jo and bring him to the warehouse. Make sure you all are dressed for the occasion because things might get a little messy".

"Aight Drew, around what time do you want all this done by?"

"Well try to have everything set and ready within the next 2 hours, I'll be there waiting".

"I got you covered my dude, you can for sure count on me".

Making his way out the front door, he turned towards me and said, "You my dog Drew, I love you baby boy. High Rollaz for life".

After Abdul left, I made my way to the kitchen to check my stash of utensils I had placed in a compartment under the sink. Upon retrieving the stash, I pulled out my weapons of choice, two 16inch butcher knives, a 6inch cork screw, and two rug cutters along with a box filled with surgical gloves, masks and plastic aprons.

Making my way upstairs to the bedroom, Eve laid in bed browsing through social media, what she did best. "I'll be back in a few, I just need to go sort some things out"

Planting a gentle kiss on my lips she said, "Ok hun, just try to make sure you are back in time for dinner."

"I'll make sure to be back in time baby".

After leaving home, I made a quick detour to one of my customer's travel agency over on Hertel ave to take care of some important business.

By the time I made it to the warehouse, I saw Abdul, Shizzle and Papa Smurf standing directly in front someone I presumed to be Jo Jo, taking turns hitting him repeatedly.

"This the piece a shit that tried killing me?", I asked with distain not directed at anyone in particular.

"Yea, that's him", Abdul replied.

As I approached even closer I could see the fear in his eyes. I wanted him to suffer for what he did to me and my family and I was determined to make sure that he did.

Removing the sock that was previously in his mouth I asked, "Who sent you to kill me, and why did you have to hurt Michelle?", I asked staring directly at him.

With tears streaming down the corner of his eyes from the excruciating pain he felt, he responded, "It wasn't my idea man, you gotta believe me. D was the one that sent me to kill you guys. I didn't want to do it but he told me if I didn't, he would kill me and my family. Your baby moms was just used to lure you. I'm sorry, but you just gotta believe me".

"Well you shouldn't have chose to mess with me and mines you piece a shit"

You've gotta believe me Drew, none of this was my idea, I swear"

"It's too late for all that now. It's judgement day and you are on the verge of meeting your maker".

The warehouse was located on Sycamore street at the end of a dead end. It has been shut down for a few months due to a fire that destroyed majority of the building, which made it an ideal location for our illegal activities.

"Yo Smurf, Shizzle, tie this fool up and put him in the back, so that we don't put that other piece a shit on point when he gets here"

"Aight we got you", Smurf stated as he and Shizzle picked up Jo Jo headed for the back of the warehouse.

Turning towards Abdul I said, "Yo, I'm a stand behind the door, so the second D walks in I'll just sneak up from behind and take him down"

"Just make sure you not visible at all and I'll do my part to lure him in"

"Okay son, I got you".

As I made my way behind the door, Abdul went to sit atop a bar stool next to what was left of an office desk, which was burned to a crisp from the previous fire.

I had my 357 magnum in hand ready for action, meanwhile keeping watch for our guest of honor. My palms were sweaty and my heart raced uncontrollably.

Within minutes, I noticed a black BMW convertible pulling into the parking lot. Seconds later D emerged from the car heading in the direction of the entrance. Turning momentarily to Abdul I motioned that D had arrived.

At that very moment, all the hate I had built up for this man was urging me to empty my gun in his chest right then and there; but I couldn't give him an easy way out. I wanted him to suffer, I wanted him to get a dose of his own medicine.

As he approached the door he turned around scanning the area to ensure he wasn't be watched or followed. This was a routine we all adopted as a way to cover our asses.

He then pushed open the door, yelling "Abdul, where you at?".

I knew if I didn't act now, my plans would possibly end up backfiring on me. With precision, I snuck up behind my target, gun butting him twice in the head, causing him to fall effortlessly to the ground.

With his gloves back on, Abdul made his way over helping me to transfer D's now unconscious body to a lawn chair we had stationed to the left of the building.

To ensure he was completely subdued, we stripped him naked, leaving him with only his socks on while using duct tape to limit his moments.

"Go get the others to come join the party", I said to Abdul with a sinister smile on my face.

In the meantime, I went to go retrieve my bag of goodies. I then emptied the contents on to a partially burnt desk located a few feet away. My adrenaline was now racing at

150 miles per hour. I have heard so many times that two wrongs don't make it right; but in this case it sure as hell did.

The first thing I did was put on a pair of surgical gloves along with my mask and apron. I knew for a fact this was going to be messy and I needed to ensure that nothing was left behind to pinpoint me to this.

Seconds later Abdul returned with both Shizzle and Smurf in tow, carrying Jo Jo's battered and motionless body bounded to a chair.

"Yo fellas, sit that bastard Jo Jo right next to his bitch ass boss, and strip him naked. Make sure to keep your gloves on, then come over here and get a pair of these". I said, pointing towards the aprons and masks I had placed on the desk.

I was determined to have these motherfuckers pay dearly, and I was for sure going to enjoy every minute of it.

"Get the hell up you piece a shit, wake up", I shouted repeatedly as I slapped D in the face causing him to regain consciousness. When he finally opened his eyes, he looked up at me and I could tell instantly that he was petrified. The look on his face gave the impression he had just seen a ghost.

I immediately began having flashbacks, seeing Michelle's lifeless body slumped over in that kitchen. This only intensified my rage, causing me to unleash the beast from within I had no idea existed.

Making my way to the table I retrieved the 16 inch butcher knives and stood in front Jo Jo. Fear now resonated in their eyes along with the uncertainty of what was to come.

Retribution was now. Reaching between Jo Jo's legs I grabbed a hold of his penis and began cutting at his testicles, causing him to squirm in sheer agony. The gloves I had on were now covered with blood as I dropped Jo Jo's manly organs to the floor. Making my way over to D, I stared in his eyes for a few seconds and asked, "Why did you have to kill her D, why didn't you leave them out of this?".

This piece of shit had the nerve to shake his head as to imply he didn't have anything to do with it. Even before death he wasn't man enough to own up to his wrong doings.

"You know what D, I hope you burn in hell". I wanted him to suffer a little while longer, so I turned to Abdul and said, "I want you guys to carve these motherfuckers up, have some fun but make sure you do a good job at it".

For the next few minutes, we took turns slicing and dicing their bodies, ensuring no part was left unattended.

By the time we were done, there was blood everywhere with skin and flesh particles scattered around their lifeless bodies. It still didn't feel like it was enough even with Jo Jo's penis lodged in D's mouth. For good measure I positioned myself in front D, lunging forward with cork screw in hand, pulling out chunks of flesh and arteries simultaneously.

.

"Yo let's hurry up and get the hell out of here fellas, and make sure to back track your every move to ensure no evidence is left behind.

To the left of me was a container marked FLAMMABLE, I motioned to Smurf to bring it over. I then went ahead and poured gasoline all over their lifeless bodies. "This is for you Mich" I whispered to myself before dropping the container to the floor.

Redirecting my attention to Abdul I said, Let's get out of here while we still can".

On our way out, I retrieve my tools and made it to the door. Before making my exit, I reached into my pocket pulling out a pack of matches.

"I hope you two burn in hell" I said before dropping the lit match directly on D's lap, causing he and Jo Jo's body to instantly become engulfed in flames.

CHAPTER 33

When we made it outside we all agreed to meet up at the spot over on Minnesota.

The first thing on my agenda was to get rid of the murder weapons and the other items we used. I decided to make a quick stop at my boys welding shop in Southside Queens.

Upon arrival, I saw him standing out front, so I walked up to him and gave him $500 and told him I needed to his melting pot. This wasn't the first time I made use of his services, so he already knew what the deal was.

For the next couple minutes, I stood in front the melting pot, dropping in each item one by one.

When I was satisfied all the evidence was correctly disposed of, I made my way over to the car wash on Adelphi to have my car detailed.

By the time I got to the spot in Southside, everyone was already there awaiting my arrival. After greeting them, I told them to sit so we could address the situation at hand.

Making sure I had everyone's undivided attention I said, "All three of you dudes sitting in this room are the future of this organization. What we just took part in will stay on the top of your minds for years to come. This shows how money can come between friends and even family; and how the same nigga you trust with your life and your loved one's lives can be the same one to turn on you. If any of you get the slightest inclination some snake shit is going down, make sure to address that situation asap. Now for the reason I called this meeting. As of today, I will be on a small hiatus for a few weeks. Shit after all this I for sure need a vacation, na mean"

We all shared a hearty laugh at my expense with that comment.

"So while I am gone, Abdul will be in charge of the entire operation. Smurf and Shizzle, I'm appointing you two as Lieutenants. With D out the picture, we are se t to lose 30% of our revenue, but in time we will be able to find a resolution for that".

"You know we got you Kid", Abdul stated as both Smurf and Shizzle confirmed his statement saying, "For sure".

"If by chance you need to get in contact with me, just holla at Abdul and he will let me know. Smurf and Shizzle, y'all family now and I need you to always remember that. High Rollaz for life my G's. We all we got. Anything y'all need don't be afraid to ask, if I got it you got it".

Getting up from where I sat, I walked over to each of them given them daps before making my exit. I needed to go spend some time with my wife to be and enjoy our little vacation in Jamaica. Kingston Jamaica, here I come.